guttersnaps

short, short pulp stories for
short, short attention spans

volume one

by
Ramzi S. Hajj

MONTAG

Montag Press Team:
Editor - Brandon Nolta
Cover Photo - Sofia Sforza
Cover Design - Steven Unzicker
Interior Photos - Ramzi S. Hajj

A Montag Press Book
www.montagpress.com
Montag Press
777 Morton Street, Unit B
San Francisco CA 94129 USA

Two kinds of trouble in this world
Living, dying

Lindsey Buckingham

Alongside decayed roués with dubious means
of subsistence and of dubious origins, alongside ruined and adventurous offshoots of
the bourgeoisie, were vagabonds, discharged
soldiers, discharged jailbirds, escaped galley
slaves, swindlers, mountebanks, lazzaroni,
pickpockets, tricksters, gamblers, pimps,
brothel keepers, porters, literati, organ grinders, ragpickers, knife grinders, tinkers, beggars
– in short, the whole indefinite, disintegrated
mass, thrown hither and thither, which the
French call la bohème.

Karl Marx

Oh sinnerman, where you gonna run to?

Nina Simone

Dedication

◆ ◆ ◆

To Team Scrimp. Always We Four.

Acknowledgment

◆ ◆ ◆

A soul-felt thank you to Steven M. Unzicker for years of friendship so deeply rooted in ideas, words, and images.

Table of Contents

◆ ◆ ◆

FRANCIS XAVIER
CHAPEL

FRANCIS XAVIER CHAPEL
PANESE CATHOLIC CENTER
ESTABLISHED 1912

All are Welcome!

Weekdays: 12:05 p.m.
Saturday Vigil: 5:00 p.m.
Sunday: 8:30 a.m.
                10:00 a.m. English
ssion: Sundays   9:30 a.m. – 9:50 a.m.

Welcoming All Lost Souls

The Power and The Glory, Revisited

♦ ♦ ♦

The archbishop had his cock out before the heavy door *snicked* shut behind me. He was standing beside his desk, smiling like an old invalid waiting on a treat.

"Uh-uh, Your Grace. I'm not the one. Your boy's been sent away."

I shifted the pistol to my left hand and pointed with my right. "You can put that away."

The archbishop fumbled with his driftwood and tucked it back into his robes. He stowed his smile, too. He never took his eyes off of me.

I moved toward the incredibly ornate table at the center of the room. I ran my fingertips along the shiny smooth surface. I checked them for dust. Not a speck. "What kind of wood is this, Your Eminence?"

He didn't answer. I pointed the piece in his direction. "It's mahogany," he said. I nodded. I reached into my jacket pocket and removed a clear glass vial. I placed it on the table. "Know what this is?" He looked at the white powder mounded behind the glass. He shook his head. "Strychnine. Bitter and unpleasant. Fast to the finish, though. A real workhorse." He seemed unimpressed.

We stood looking at each other. Seven feet apart, no more. From my other pocket, I placed a short drinking glass and small bottle of water alongside the vial of strychnine.

"You've … ah … really done a number on a lot of people. A lot of people. You remember Zachary Benoit?" He nodded. "Older brother of mine. Used to be a good older brother. He's in Joliet now. Killed two people. Just shot 'em down in a hotel room. Then sat in a chair. Can you believe that?" He shook his head. "Me neither. I wonder what made him kill those two guys. Hell, he paid them to come to his room. Do you wonder?"

No answer. I took two giant steps toward him, gun in my right hand, pointed at his head.

"No!"

"*No* is right. The whole world knows *no* is right. You called the defense lost and misguided for trying to pin the blame on you. You got a right, sure. Can't prove anything from twenty-five years ago. Just sat tight and prayed for their misguided and lost souls."

"It wasn't me."

"Sure it's been you. There's a line of former boys a mile long waiting to have at you for their recompensation that says it's you." I looked around the room. "And here you still are in this fine old house."

He looked around his room.

"What kind of repentance we doing tonight?"

He stood looking at me.

"Here. I'll get your thoughts going. *You have plowed wickedness, you have reaped injustice, you have eaten the fruit of lies.* Where's that one from?"

He closed his eyes for a moment. "Hosea 10:13."

I nodded and pointed the gun at him. "Your turn."

He took a deep breath. "*Create in me a clean heart, O God, and put a new and right spirit within me. Do not cast me away from your presence, and do not take your holy spirit from me. Restore to me the joy of your salvation, and sustain in me a willing heart. Amen.*"

"Nice. I've heard that one before."

"Psalm 51:10. I can share another if you'd like."

I looked at him awhile, trying to imagine what remorse would sound like. "You people love your words and mantras. You sure do. Useless. All of it. Forget it. Don't worry about sharing anything."

But I wanted him to worry about many things. He deserved nothing less.

"I suppose to you people our obvious choices here are suicide and *your* immortal soul, or murder and *my* immortal soul."

"Yes."

"Quite the conundrum, I guess. But then again ... do you get the impression I give a shit about my immortal soul, Padre?"

"One ought tend..."

I started to raise my gun.

"No."

"I tell you what, then. I'm thinking a little Sacrament of the Penance here can go a long way. A grand act of confessional penance. You can deputize me your father confessor to keep things nice and kosher. Your redemption ... will be in saving *both* our immortal souls. A selfless act God will surely smile upon. In his infinite mercy. So beautiful."

He looked blankly at me.

"And that's your third and final option, Daddy-O. I'm counting to ten in my head, then we're going with the second option. In the groin."

"What do you want me to say?"

"The truth. Of what you did to Zachary. Start to finish. Six. Seven."

"I can do that."

"Bully. Let's start." I sat down in a plush armchair. He remained standing.

He cleared his throat.

I took out my phone and pointed the camera at him. "I'm ready when you are, Your Holiness." As a show of faith, I placed the gun on the wide armrest.

He stared at me, or at the pinhole eye of the camera lens. I watched him on the screen. I imagined he was ordering his mind. My thumb hovered over the red Record button. I felt I could wait a long time.

He couldn't. He ambled to his impressively shiny and dustless mahogany table. He unscrewed the cap off the plastic bottle. He poured water into the glass. Halfway. He uncapped the vial and tapped the strychnine out of the vial into the glass of water and reciprocated my show of faith.

Holding On

Mother Lode

◆ ◆ ◆

There's a real humdinger of an insult from the mountains of Lebanon (I think) that translates into something like "you son of she who pisses without squatting."

It's a strong visual.

Yeah, well, the son? That's me.

Finding titty pics of my mother on the internet is a pretty easy thing to do. My friends are obsessed with finding, collecting, and sharing these pics. That's how we were raised, on a steady diet of internet porn. Titty pics. Pussy pics. Straight fuck pics. Dick-in-mouth pics. Sorority girl-on-girl pics… pics of her pissing on a sidewalk, standing in a puddle of her own urine (yes, there are more than one).

And selfies.

Always with the selfies.

The five years she spent at Arizona State University getting a communications degree were well-lived, well-documented. Her tramp stamp inked into the small of her back reads *All Deliveries in the Front*. The words are underscored by a fancy, double-sided arrow. It's a real work of art.

You get the picture.

It's also a bit of a moot point now. My mother has inoperable brain cancer. It's just one of those things. She's only thirty-eight. She's wasting away, like she's deleting herself.

It's been just the two of us since forever. And I still don't know what to think of her.

Into the Vortex

Damage Done

◆ ◆ ◆

The thing was, he burned that boy of his with lit cigarettes. All along the underside of his arm, back behind his elbow. Sometimes in his armpits. He hurt that boy something terrific.

It wasn't a thing with rage, sadism, or booze. There was conscientiousness to his actions. It hurt him to hurt his boy. He told the boy as much. He wanted him to be a better boy, to obey the time-honored traditions of fathers and sons. *Don't you see what I'm trying to tell you. Don't you feel it?* The boy felt it, but didn't see it. Not yet. And the pox of burns multiplied.

Now the boy has a boy, and the father a grandson. There are no new burns, only the lore of burns. And the grandson is well-versed in the tactility of lore, and no longer shy to run his finger along his father's arm to connect the memories. *I am deeply disappointed. I know you know better.* He extends his arm and the boy runs his finger along its length. Back and forth. It's his moral education and inheritance. The grandfather looks on wordlessly, the stoic, wondering what the boy will show his boy.

So, when the grandfather is found dead in his recliner, and the son eulogizes him at length at the gravesite in searing August heat, the boy looks up at his father with wetness in his eyes. The salt burns. He wipes at them with his short tie. His father glances at him, not breaking his cadence, smiles, and rubs his arm in reminder, tribute, remembrance, and a pride that sees into the distance.

Way of the Alley

Defenestration

◆ ◆ ◆

I dropped Joe, Jr. out the window. I weigh north of 320 and he clocked in around 170. I physically picked him up in my arms and took him to the window. That's what I'm paid to do. He yowled and squirmed like a little baby cradled in my arms. Made no difference. I shoved my laden arms through the open window and dropped him. He fell the seven stories like a misshapen sausage in a vacuum. Straight and true. No fuss, no muss from atmospheric resistance. Pure gravity. Straight and true. The last sound that slimy fuck made before his watermelon-for-a-head hit the pavement was something expected from an angry, cornered wolf. It was frightening. Nobody wants to die like that. I understand that. I'm not a psychopath.

I picked up his wallet off the floor. Opened it. And there stared at me a little girl of, maybe, five. Wearing a cardboard birthday crown. Holding a giant sunflower by the stalk. Wearing a shirt that read "I [heart] my Daddy."

"Oh, for heaven's sake."

I slide the picture out. I tossed the wallet out after Joe, Jr. I kept the picture. The wailing of sirens in the distance was my cue to get my tender-hearted caboose to vamoose.

I parked along the curb outside 861 Acorn and got out. Joe Jr.'d done okay with himself. Nice house. Neat lawn. Nothing to get suspicious about. I walked the red brick path to the door. I knocked through a nice-smelling pine branch Christmas wreath. The door opened and an older woman in a housecoat stood looking at me.

"Yeah?"

I took the picture out of my coat pocket. "Is this girl here at this house?"

Her eyes darted at the picture. Then back. "Fuck'r you, fatso?"

"Lady, I just want to give this back to her. She live here?"

"If you think for one fat second I'd answer that question, you're stupider than you look."

"Here, then take it." I held it out to her.

"I'm taking no nothing from some wormy fat pre-vert. In fact –" She reached for something that clanged against a hollow-sounding metal something else. I had my pistol out, pressed hard against her heart, and the chamber emptied before she shifted the aluminum bat to her right hand. She dropped fast. The bat bounced and clanged on the tiled floor.

"For fuck's sake."

I pushed her back into the house with my foot. She slid across the blood-slicked floor nicely. I kicked the bat in after her. I closed the door. I tucked the picture back in with the gun.

Just one of those days.

The neighborhood was quiet. No one in sight. No sounds arriving from anywhere else. A nice winter's day. The nippy air smelled nice.

In the car, I lit a cigarette and tried to remember the last time I'd used that gun. It had been a while. A long while. I started the car and got out of there.

The Robinsons Are There

Words > Stick + Stone

◆ ◆ ◆

In the United States, according to a recent study, a certain insidious word is, on average, spoken or thought of over one hundred million times per day. Every day. Maybe it's a bit less on Christmas Day, but it is surely made up for throughout the month of February. It's a powerful word, this word. It's a mindset, an evocation of peculiar things in times past, a hierarchal affirmation that, no matter what, the utterer maintains certain inalienable rights that no shifting socio-economic or moral mores can ever erase. *I may be poor, but I'm not that.* There is an abiding power in this word, a faith. And Powerless people are always in the market for "empower-ment," no matter the quality of the product offered. And the "empowerment" market will never have demand-side softness (the derivatives market for its many euphemisms is heavily traded, too). It's how these things work.

⌒o⌒

When the responding officers responded to the call of a sin-gle shot fired on the seventh floor of Booker Public Housing

19

Building D, they found one Kendrick Pope in his studio apartment, dead on the floor from an (apparent) self-inflicted gunshot wound to the head. The tall cop poked Kendrick in the side with the toe of his boot. "These fucking people. Couldn't find someone else to shoot so he got itchy and shot himself."

∽o∾

At first, I thought someone had farted on my fantasies. I was pissed. Upon closer inspection, I realized someone had shit on my fantasies. I was apoplectic. I hit the wall. I made a hole in the plaster. My knuckles still ache. A lot of things don't matter anymore in this country. That's why our fiction is so piss-poor. Nobody wants to listen to someone else's crazy-ass stories. All we have—really—are delusions, deeply held superstitions, and preconceived notions. But at least they're all ours. We can no longer trace the paternity of the junk ideas we buy. They just are, as if they've always been. And if one man starts shitting in another's temple of sacred relics and ruminations, bad things start to happen. It's how civil wars start. It's how Liberals get their comeuppance. It's how a lot of [you know *whos*] get called [you know *whats*], get beat, tased, dragged behind fast-moving cars on rutted dirt roads, shot. All is fair game. It's like love.

∽o∾

There's no racism. There is an ether of classism through which we move where the dumb shits get taken advantage of by the not-so-dumb shits. If, say, someone gets you all dewy-eyed and primes your gears to vote against your own economic self-interest by waving a Bible, a gun, a giant butterfly net to be used on people who don't look like you, and it's all typeset in an illustrated brochure printed circa 1955, then you're a dumb shit. And you will get taken every time. Count on it. So, you're told to sit back, shut up, don't worry, and we'll come looking for you when your vote is needed again. In the meantime, go play with some opioids. I hear carfentanil is quite pleasant. It's an elephant tranquilizer.

∽o∾

May 28, 1957, was the very last time Mr. Calhoun called me a "young buck." He'd been talking to Mr. Carlisle Ellis about how surprisingly efficient I'd become as his stock boy. He thought I had a real chance of becoming an assistant to the assistant manager. His words that day I have placed in a special memory compartment—the words, the diction, the volume: "This young buck here is something else. If he keeps his snout clean and his pecker dry, he's going places. Isn't that right, Frankie?" I was standing two paces to his left.

Well, fuck you very much, Mr. Calhoun.

The very next day, I packed two bags, took the money Ms. Lilly was holding for me, kissed her on the cheek, and went to the bus station. I bought a ticket to Pascagoula, and from there to Chicago.

In Chicago, I went to the Social Security Administration building and got a new name and new number.

As Mr. Francisco Vargas, I went to a library branch on South State Street and borrowed two books on Cuban history.

As a hardscrabble Caribbean immigrant, I did lots of things. I kept my nose in my own business. I worked hard. I built things. I saved money. I went places.

I married the lovely Marie, wet my pecker, and had the even lovelier Rochelle.

And now, I'm sitting in a pew with Marie in Rockefeller Chapel at the University of Chicago waiting for our Rochelle to receive her degree in chemistry. She'll be going to California to do her graduate work. She, too, will do lots of things.

What are You Trying to Say?

Pulp, Self-Conscious

◆ ◆ ◆

It's tricky, but in the end, when it comes, the only thing that'll have mattered will probably be love—the giving and receiving of it. It's important to keep the giving and receiving of love at as stable an equilibrium as possible to avoid an encounter with someone like me. I'm not a bad man, not in the strictest definition of the word, not in my mind, not in the mind of those who are left to me, not by the actions that precede me. I'm a bad man because I know what I do is not the right thing. The wrong thing. There are no redeeming virtues to my labors. I judge other people's actions, document their lack of fealty, destroy whatever shred of civility that may remain between two people, collect my money, go home. I have no unnatural attachment to money, it's a comfortable subsistence-plus arrangement. My expenses are meticulously documented, my time valued with a reasonable markup, with no room for an inflated sense of importance. My clients tell me they appreciate that. And I tell them I appreciate prompt payments. They have the luxury of being late with my money exactly one time. I tell them that, too. There are no problems here. The problems are out there.

This is my introduction, my calling card, as they pass through my door into the shadows they think I live in. Sit down, please. You may call me Lance, or Mr. Boyle, or nothing at all. Your choice. Then an attentive silence from me. The unraveling of a life unfolds before me—duplicity, depravity, avarice, retribution, punishment, humiliation… weakness. There is very, very little variation. I've taken my notes, gauged the complexity and time commitment, quoted a minimum fee. There can be no further action on my part prior to a twenty percent retainer fee hitting my till. I can wait no longer than midweek next week. My apologies. I answer questions patiently—and they have many—then ease them out of the office and into a damp San Francisco morning. We are then each alone with our reflections.

I swivel into my solitude, the chair creaking under my reclined weight, gazing out the window through a fast-moving mist onto the bay and its gray bridge, living the cliché happily, wondering about other men in other times, real and fictional. There is no mystery, nor romance, nor glory to the grayscale world of operatives, maybe the second oldest profession, maybe developed to keep the ledgers on the oldest. I try not to waste time abstracting my reality unduly, although I'd like to believe I have all the time in the world.

Most prospects return on their own impatient volitions, re-darken the doorway with less hesitancy, ease themselves back into the chair opposite me, place the cash retainer reverently on the desk, wait for a physical accounting which doesn't come, ready themselves to further elaborate on their injustices upon request. It's a one-sided prompted conversation of love worn and done. I have nothing to add or subtract. I take what's given. It's what I work with. Movements, habits, tastes, compulsions, suspicions, missing money, misplaced trust, the list could continue—the human condition is embedded in the strains of our relationships, what had once been hoped for, what it had become. Decisions made and regretted, abandoned and resuscitated, only to be abandoned again, never reaching me in their flowering. It's the only way I've come to imagine it. For the most part, we seem incapable of divining poor character from good for reasons that perpetually defy. Maybe hopefulness, maybe ignorance, maybe naïveté. Have I been jilted of fees and good graces? Most certainly. Lied to, manipulated, duped? Without a doubt. There is no lasting shame attached, a lesson learned, repeated later in a different incarnation. A piece of the whole. The connection between any two people may just as easily be wedded to fallacy and avarice as to truth and honor. It is as natural as the connection itself. There is no point in justifying yourself and your actions to me, just as there is no sanity in vilifying the other. I have already taken sides, and here is your receipt. It is a part of the original parcel, you getting to me before the other. What you want from me, I say, is the anecdotal confirmation of what you allege. Correct?

Yes.

Thank you for your time. I'll be in touch with regular updates and invoices.

We move in the open, most of us observed, but not remembered. I am paid to watch and remember. To be found and recorded is simplicity personified. There are no secret places, there have never been any secret places. Even your thoughts are betrayed by your actions. You are nowhere at any time, just as surely as you are somewhere at all times. This is neither abstraction, nor empty words. This is what a man like me does, at the behest of someone who may have once loved you.

Orwell, Shelved

This Man Orwell

◆ ◆ ◆

1947. He'd been sick, getting sicker. It was in the air. The England he knew wasn't faring much better. Victory from victory pure chimera. Peace from war pure chimera. They were tired. Worn. The Continent? Forget it. Desolation. Ruin. Hunger. And Joe Stalin still wiping the soles of his boots of the viscera wedged in the treads. The sick man scratched pencil to paper, stringing forth words like a pox upon the future. Somewhere in the future—randomly, 1984—something big and bad and untoward was bound to happen by then. Surely.

He'd seen that crank Franco, the pernicious Uncle Joe Stalin, that crazed arsonist Hitler. The savage buffoonery of Benito. Sooner or later, the learned men who fancied themselves leaders of other, less learned men were going to get talked into something from which there would be no return because there would no longer be anyone to put up the treasure and the blood to make things right.

Words. Such power. Words to images. Images to action. Action to results. Results codified as law. Laws changed with the force of wordless bullets. Meaningless words. Propaganda.

Then no more laws. No more words to conjure new images. Stasis. Status quo. Rot and degradation. Yes. Yes. This is all quite possible.

He opened his hand and let the pencil roll out across the desk. He closed his eyes. He was tired. He tried to think back to India days. How easy it had been for so few little men with guns like himself to master the situation. It was falling apart now, of course. Because of the war. The victor defeated. And he could be happy for the freedom of so many people. The cost would be high and bloody and a cynical status quo would follow. He felt certain of that much. He wanted to sigh.

It hurt to breathe.

He reached across the desk for the pencil. He took it to the paper and scrawled *fear above man*. He put a line through those three words. Then *ignorance above man*. He watched those three words dance across his paper. Ignorance as birthright and religion. Ignorance as meaning. Ignorance as strength.

Then he said in shallow monotone, "I'm fearful because I'm ignorant. I'm ignorant because I'm fearful."

He wasn't afraid to die. He drank water, and ate next to nothing, and smoked cigarettes to prove it to himself. He wasn't going to miss living, *per se*, as much as he was going to miss having his ideas. And the words to explain the ideas. Not that the dead missed anything. He'd been on this god-forsaken, rain-soaked island for six months, living off the dankness like mold. This cottage smelled like the hovels he knew in England, France, Spain. It smelled of penury and defeat.

He was poor and losing, but still fighting. He knew his words could stand in his stead, if only he could keep them moving forward on the double-quick toward whatever truths he could find. He imagined a world getting bigger, bigger, bigger, with responsibilities getting heavier, heavier, heavier, and men feeling themselves to becoming smaller, smaller, smaller, all the while reaching for something akin to a womb. There could be no hiding from what had come before. There could be no rejection of the harvest of history any more than there could be a rejection of the harvest of the atom. It was a trajectory despite protestations and willful ignorance. Real power would be grasped by men who arrested the trajectory, shaped it, used it like a play thing. Control the past, control the future; control the present, control the past. A clean equation.

He'd seen the three horsemen.

He'd already seen war sold as peace.

He held men in disdain for sloughing off their bare skins of freedom for the cloaks of slavery.

And now he knew how ignorance becomes bliss, comfort, strength.

The gutter rats like himself would have no chance at all, none, none, not that the roof rats would fare any better, their loftier vistas notwithstanding. It was getting late for them all. Old ideas lay slain, rotting to bone, in nearly neat rows on a field stretching to the curvature of the earth. The slain had been pals of his. Not that ideas could be trusted anymore, tens of millions of newly dead people attesting so posthumously. Most of the living were tired and vulnerable. The idyll days of simple youth exerted their pull, and he gathered it was such a thing that fed gruel to the strong to render them weak and servile. He knew *vigilance* was no longer an operative word. He felt an innate need to try to explain what would take its place. He thought of yet another man with promises. He'd been thinking about that one great man and his promises, the one man who would find it easy to make free men his tools. He would tell that particular story. It would be his posterity.

He didn't want to waste any more time. He squinted at the page and tried to imagine penning the one hundred thousand words or so that he knew were collecting in the top bowl of the hourglass, already escaping through narrow neck, collecting, one by one, on the blank page. He felt time move. Tick. Tick. Tick.

He angled the pencil's tip against the paper and wrote: *It was a bright cold day in ~~March~~ April and the clocks were striking thirteen.*

Missing

American Military Logic

◆ ◆ ◆

"**Y**ou're lucky, Lieutenant."

"Oh yeah? How's that, Doc?"

"Being limbless, you can't hold on to the past."

The lieutenant nodded appreciatively.

"You're lucky, too, Doc."

"That's good to know. How so for me?"

"If I had one finger remaining on one hand on one arm, I'd shoot you between the fucking eyes for saying shit like that. Sir."

Dr. Falkenhyn etched notes into his notebook with his fountain pen.

"That does make us both lucky."

Crazy City, Man

Cheeses!

◆ ◆ ◆

I hand-carve Jesus figurines and larger statues from various types of cheese blocks. Mostly for weddings, *quinceañeras*, and baptisms. It relaxes me. Brings me closer to God. It's a true labor of love.

I started off in my kitchen, taking orders mostly from friends and friends of friends, in a strictly off the books, wink-wink, under the table, what-the-health-department-don't-know-won't–hurt-'em type of setup. Business got better. People I didn't know started calling up. People were asking if I was planning on having a website. I had to go legit. I had the money. Not a problem. I thought I'd call the company "Cheeses Christ, Inc." Catchy. Memorable. The name got around. People liked it. Thought it edgy, clever. Then I was visited by a Pettoruti family member I'd never seen before. He politely requested I reconsider the name. It offended his family's sensibilities, he told me. Any other name I could think of would be fine. Within reason, of course. They'd let me know if they disapprove, just to be on the safe side.

I gave it quite a bit of thought and settled on "Holy Cheeses, Inc." People liked that one, too.

Then I waited. Maybe two weeks.

No one came back with any complaints of sensibilities offended.

I filed the incorporation papers.

Nativity

Something Akin
to Something Else

◆ ◆ ◆

Nothing. Rolling earth. Undulating grain. Wind. Sun. Nothing that could do him any good. He feels needful. He touches the empty bottle. He rests his head against the brick wall. He waits on the goodwill of strangers.

A Datsun pickup drives slowly down the street. Slows. Stops. "Low Cloud!"

The man looks up at the sound of his name. Smiles a familiar, mostly toothless smile at the man draped through the open window. His hands are huge against the door. "You need work today, Low Cloud?"

"Naw. Not today. Today I'm busy."

The man in the idling pickup looks at him, then off into the Nebraska sky. The sun is still low. "It's going to be a real scorcher today. You be OK?"

"Sure. Jesus provides."

"Sure he does. You take it easy now."

"Sure. I'll take it easy."

The pickup drives away. The street is empty again. Low Cloud stares off into whatever distance he can see. Two, three hundred years ago, he might have been a different man. There would have been no street, no bottle. And no Pine Ridge reservation. The Oglala Sioux would have been out there where his eyes were blurring the horizon—riding, hunting, warring, loving, living, dying. Two, three hundred years ago is a long time, collective memory reduced to myth, folklore, flogged cliché. Nothing sustainable. Nothing re-creatable. Nothing to lift the low on high. Just something once was.

A battered Ford Aerostar van clatters along the street. Stops. A sunny woman at the wheel. The side door grinds open along its worn, dented tracks. A young man peers out. "Low Cloud, my man."

He pushes off the ground. Approaches the open door.

"Where to today?"

"Today's a short day. The creek for a swim, lunch, back here. A coupla hours."

"Sure. I like that."

He climbs in. The door grinds shut. The van clatters off.

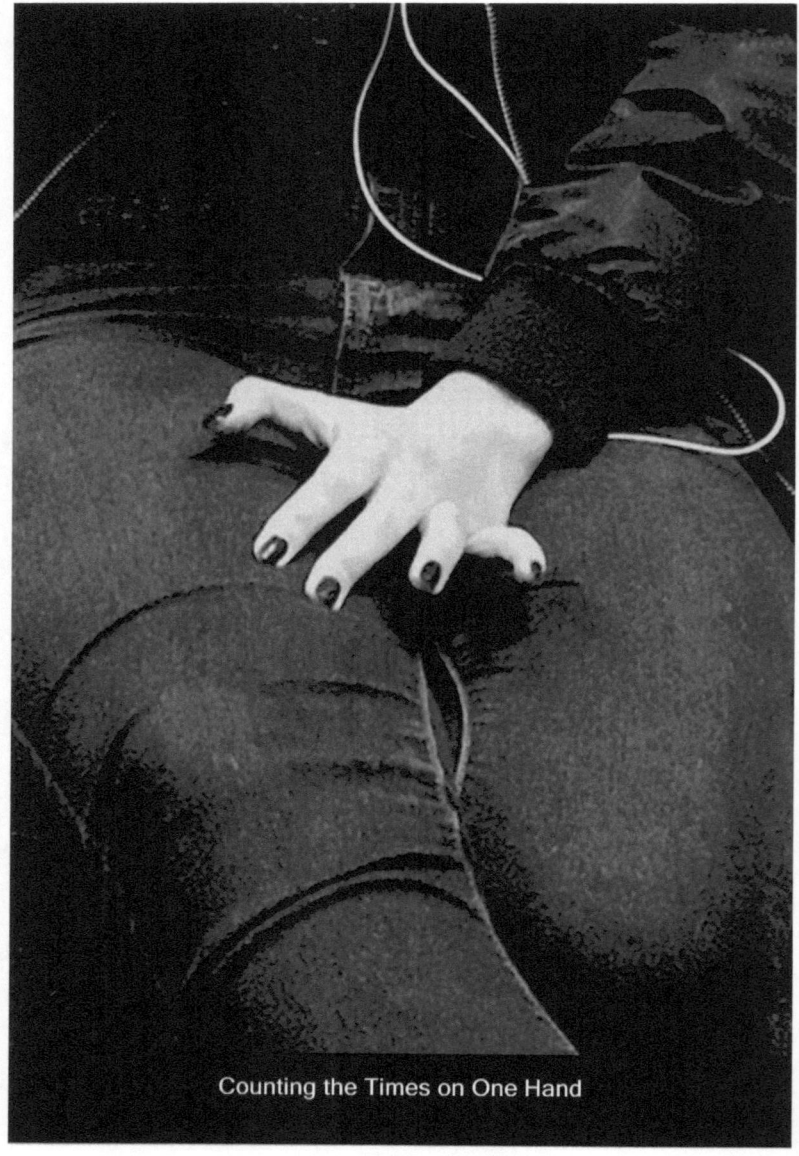

Counting the Times on One Hand

Basic Math

◆ ◆ ◆

Something wasn't right. She was in a frenzy, working my cock like a diabetic works one of those sugar-free lollipops. I wasn't having these thoughts when it was happening. These thoughts came later. This is by no means a gripe session. But here's the rub: Two weeks ago—to the day—I couldn't get her lips and tongue to coordinate a kind word to the Good Reverend Jimmy. That was the morning right before I took her to LAX for an Alitalia flight to Rome.

I was afraid of putting two and two together, for fear I'd end with five and have to spend thirty-five to life someplace for doing something stupid. My jealousy was going to get a workout. Maybe even stretched to the limit. My pride and ego were going to have a rough go. But I still had to know how she came by these phenomenal fellatio skills. Even the fucking word sounds Italian. Did they invent this thing? Do they have young swarthy studs meeting unsuspecting American women getting off planes at Rome International and giving the advanced courses on the art of licking the length of the shaft, working the tip, and the gentle nut sack squeeze? Good God, man. She worked me like an Amsterdam pro (don't ask).

But I digress.

I love Bethany. She's my dream girl. Proposing to her was the most natural thing. She said *yes* without hesitation. Sure, there'd been lots of prudish things about her, she'd been raised with lots of guilt and Jesus sayings, but I liked the idea of growing in that "biblical" way together. I most certainly didn't expect her to go to Rome for a two-week IT consulting project and return as the naughty girl of sorority lore. But holy lord, she's been working my joint nonstop since her return. Where do I draw the line on my indignation? Do I want her to unlearn what she's somehow learned? She believes in miracles, so I could chalk it up as an immaculate conception of a blessed oral sex nympho and feel grateful for her miracle in the process. The thought of calling it all off and letting some other guy get all of her attentions would be plain dumb. Just the thought of that approach makes my blood bubble.

It's back to the ego and the crazy, irrational thoughts. She tells me she'll be going back to Rome, possibly Milan, for more project work, maybe three or four more times over the next six to nine months, and I have no idea where my head is. The thought gnawing at my very being is that she is making pilgrimages to a place of original sins, returning to me to corrupt my immortal soul with such feelings of bitterness and anger and jealousy and vengefulness and lust. But part of the corruption feels warm and heavenly in the moment and leads me to distraction at most other times. I am of a mind to surrender myself to the workings of pleasure, and trust lust and desire to drain the swamp of vanity and vengeance. It seems the rational thing to do.

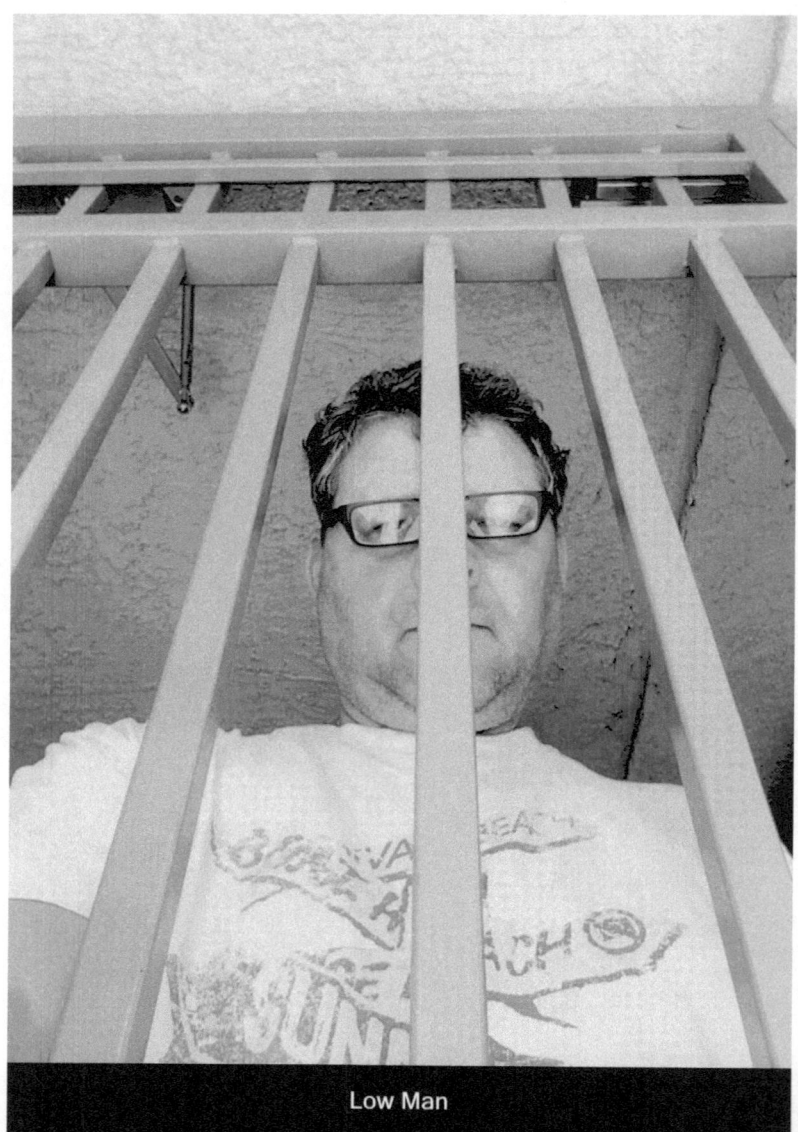

Low Man

Low Man

◆ ◆ ◆

H e tossed the borrowed copy of *Death of a Salesman* on the floor, thrust back into the couch, and sighed. He closed his eyes and did his breathing exercises, counting back from his lucky number, seventeen. He'd long since lost his lease to his happy place. Failure to keep up with payments, mostly. *My balls ache*, he thought. *The fridge is empty, I'm barely employable, and my balls ache.* He lost track of his reverse-counting somewhere before eleven. Today, like yesterday, like tomorrow. In this dump of a house. The orbs of listlessness and bad luck sucking the marrow from the bone that supports life. A continuous, disgusting slurping sound. He felt like a cadaver, useless. He sometimes wished he were dead. But he didn't have the guts to do it. He pulled the .38 Super Automatic from under the cushion. Black. Sleek. Rough grip. His heart leapt for a moment, then settled into a sweet, anticipatory rhythm. Like Christmas, or the prospect for a lubricated hand job.

A real *Whiff Lowman* he'd become. Indeed, yes. The only thing going for him at this juncture—the mildly punny word play. Time was escaping by the second into his late, late forties. No wife anymore. Kidless. Family as loving as he loved them. Nary a phone call or card to mark the occasions. Friends as faded and scattered as ambition. A job that paid some bills, but could do nothing to let the future know he was on his way. Books, booze, food, porn, sleep, guns.

He took out the Sig Sauer from under the other cushion and laid it next to its couch mate. Another real beaut, this one: chrome barrel, blood-red grip. These two had come into his life after a particularly inspiring weekend of watching *The Wild Bunch* and *Butch Cassidy and The Sundance Kid*. Going out in a (yet-to-be-determined) blaze of glory with a pistol in either hand held powerful sway through the following Monday afternoon when he plopped down his cash for his destiny. By Tuesday morning, alas … he just couldn't imagine himself being that monumental prick devastating other peoples' destinies for a fleeting moment of glory, psychological comeuppance, and a reviled posterity.

He retrieved the book from the floor. He flipped through the pages and found his place. Biff had been saying something dickish to Willy. He re-read from a few lines above and got back into his groove. *"Pop! I'm a dime a dozen, and so are you!"* He shoved the beauts between the cushions and couch back and reclined against a pillow, turning the page.

Opacity

Here

◆ ◆ ◆

He stood in the open doors of the mostly empty hayloft. The smudges on the horizon swirling angry red dust along the road leading to this place? That was the past catching up with him. They were moving fast. They were taking a chance on him still being here. He was in an obliging mood.

He couldn't remember the last time he hadn't been running. Sure, he'd stayed in places for a while, even had himself a woman in a real domesticated setting once or twice. He had a kid someplace, a boy—sure. But it had always been part of something else, like being someone else entirely. Not now. Not here. Not anymore. This was it.

The promises he had broken were on their way. For all he was concerned, every lie he ever told were in those shining metal boxes on wheels, kicking up that red dust. They were coming. He could almost smell the dirt in the air. He could taste something metallic—like blood. His fingers went down the length of the leather holster flush against his left flank. Its familiarity gave him a certain comfort. Now was the time for comfort.

He paced the floor. His hard bootheel echoes marked time off the walls. He squatted by a body on the floor, searching its pockets for cigarettes. Nothing. He turned on his heel and did the same with the other body. Nothing. He stood and moved back to the open loft doors. The fast-moving reddish smears were closer, larger. He wanted to see sun glinting off the metal and glass. For dramatic effect. He squinted. Nothing. He leaned against the doorframe and wished for a cigarette.

Whoever was coming was going to get shot at. Fourteen times. Maybe thirty times. No more. It would depend on several different things. The men on the floor had been unarmed. Useless. He looked down at the truck parked off the barn door. Here's the deal he cut with himself: *If I make it out of this thing, I'm going to take that truck, drive to California, rob a bank in Santa Monica, drive to Alaska, buy a boat, sail it down to Seattle, settle down into something, and do my damnedest not to be here again.*

And if not, he wouldn't know the difference.

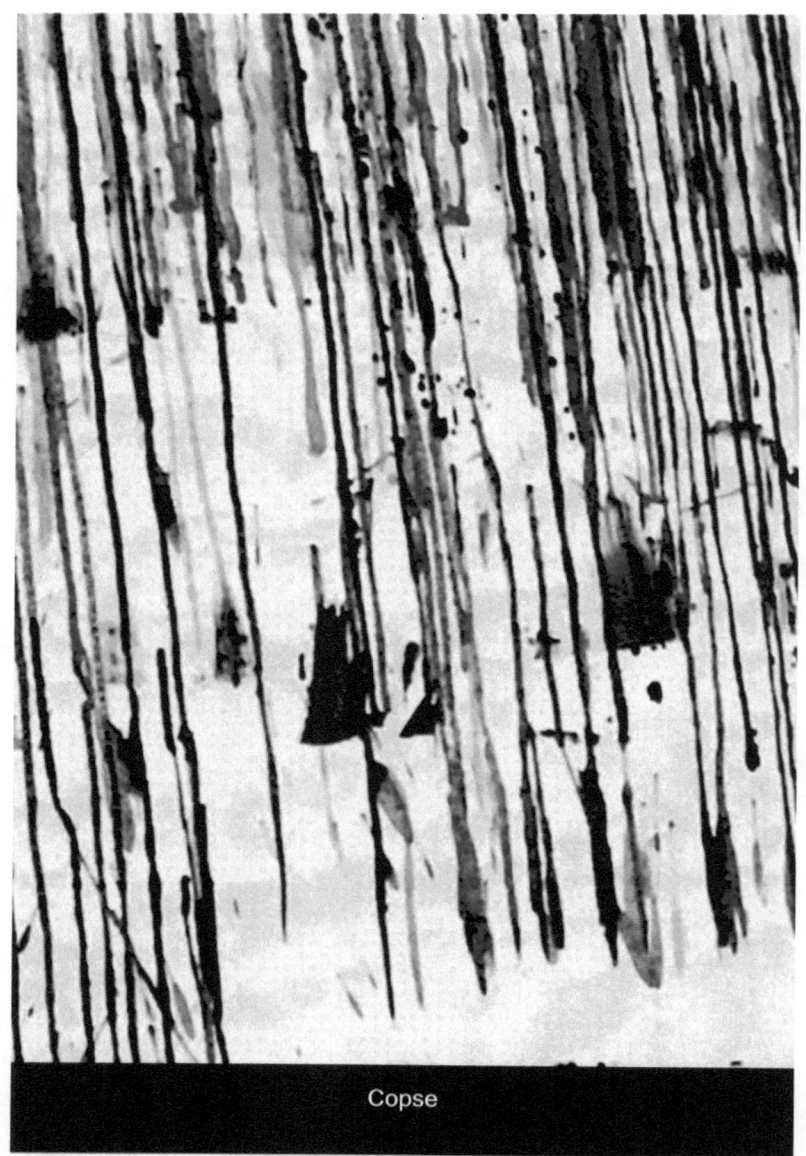

Copse

The Wild Life

◆ ◆ ◆

We were rutting like two woodland animals in the dark, windowless underbrush that is my mother's basement. But I was thinking of something else.

If I were telling you this twenty years ago, when I was sixteen or seventeen, that would be one thing. You would've said, "Oh, you horny kids!" and moved the hell along. But that was then. This here is now, me and Sheila with not much else to do in the perpetual rutting season. We drink. We eat. We smoke. We play video games. I read while Sheila works at the A&W on the state route. She "stitches with my bitches" while I make and rip tickets and pop popcorn at the Regency second-run. We make more than enough to score a few twelve-packs every day or so, Pizza Hut for dinner, Winston Lights, some weed. The library is less than a mile away. We walk there most of the time. But we got a car. We're never light on gas. Hell, Obama gave us pretty good health insurance. Just in case. You never know. Got to be smart about these things. We save a few shekels here and there for road trips when the mood strikes. New Mexico. Oregon. Wisconsin. We send postcards to family and friends. We may live in a windowless basement, but we're not rude, selfish animals.

We keep the car in good running order.

It's not that we're stupid or lack education. We find ourselves on the other extreme, at that tiny nexus where self-awareness, something that smells like existential fatalism, and laziness meet. It's easy to reconcile. We've done it a thousand times. Like that fancy Descartes said, except our own thoughts, there is nothing absolutely in our power. So why bother? I mean, what's the point of too much effort? Mom's real generous with the basement. We're real courteous and respectful of her stuff. Even when we have guests over, they mind their Ps and their Qs, or else out they go. Inviolable house rules. We eat, drink, smoke, fuck, entertain ourselves in other ways when not fucking, get older, maybe wiser ...

But here's the thing. Todd Wilkes told me the other day he was pretty damned sure he saw Sheila giving Kurt Zeller a hand job last Friday in Kurt's car. They were in the parking lot of Gordon's Pond. Right around noon. He's the lifeguard there. And as we all learned in high school, the hand job is gateway employment to the blowjob, the deed, and beyond. So I've been assuming things these past few days.

I'm not going to get angry or crazy or anything. But I am hurt. I thought we had a good thing going, Sheila and I. A real cozy, mellow, sustainable arrangement. I mean, what else are we going to do? Who else are we going to shack up with? I'll tell you this much: Kurt Zeller has no intention of having anything to do with Sheila long term. Kurt's not a bad dude.

It's a bang-and-fling thing with him. He's like an alley cat, wild and always on the make. That's why they call him KZ. That's how it's been with him. Everyone pretty much knows that. Sheila knows that.

We all make our decisions.

I'll keep thinking on it for a while. I'm in no big-time rush, to be honest. And when I get up enough energy, I'll toss her out. She'll probably regret it, and maybe so will I. But just because I'm poor and living off the good graces of others doesn't mean I can't have myself some pride of place. I just don't want to be around ungrateful, cheating people. You are the company you keep, right?

For the time being, we're rutting like two woodland animals in the dark, windowless underbrush that is my mother's basement. We belong down here, doing what we're doing.

Waiting

Vitriol

◆ ◆ ◆

I wish murder could be legal and the dead resurrected and for time to stand still so I could kill you, have you come back, press pause on my aging, to then kill you again when you're this age again. But it's not and they don't and it won't. And so here I am, left alone in our mostly empty and quiet house with the cheap spirits and demons that can surely make me make a bad decision.

You broke my heart.

No Longer Together

The Widow Mulligan

◆ ◆ ◆

They said the Widow Mulligan looked good. They said she'd be taken real good care of, now she's a widow. The right amount of TLC, house servants, a nice cushy life. They said he said she deserved it after the unfortunate way her husband went to join the trinity. Tony Toenails himself guaranteed it. I heard him say it. They said he'd already cleared the deck of his personal life in preparation.

She looked even better to me. When I had squirrelled away "Swinging" Joe Mulligan in Fresh Kills, I had exactly zero idea what had been on the church-sanctioned receiving end of his appetites. And 'twas his appetites that had done him in. He'd banged one too many unbangables he had no business banging. He had some cojones on him, that one did. He'd banged Tony Toenail's youngest daughter. Those kind of cojones. It was nothing personal on my part. He'd been warned by TT personally. I was the price for not heeding warnings.

Back to the Widow Mulligan.

The Lord had made it sunny and warmish for Swinging Joe's funeral. And the sun was shining down in a heavenly way on the Widow Mulligan. She had this low-cut black number on. If it had been high noon, her heavy rack would have cast a shadow in an arc at her feet. Her legs were long, and bare, and tanned, and shapely and cradled an ass jutting out into space that would have made Sir Fig Newton recheck his calculations. Her stilettos made me want to slip a hundo or a million bucks into her cleavage for just one dance. Just one. She belonged on a screen in a dark room with a sticky floor. She belonged in a lot of different places. I gawked at her like a teenager at a pool club, antsily waiting on a movement, a heave, a bounce, a jiggle. I started to pray.

My porn-marinated brain was dissolving.

Mercifully, I couldn't see her face behind the black lace veil.

I took a deep breath, then started to get angry. If I had seen the Widow Mulligan before her widowhood, I may have killed Swinging Joe twice, or at the very least made him suffer more for being such an ungrateful nit. Give thanks for what you have, Joe. It would have saved you in more ways than one. No do-overs, Joe. *Snick.* It's too late now. *Snick.* You best stay dead.

I got distracted from my anger when I started feeling Mr. Jimmy Johnson was starting to scratch against the fabric of my chinos looking for an out. His attention hadn't wavered. He was wanting things he knew I wanted. But I am the one who should know better. I felt a cold panic. I thought about the Mets lineup. I thought about white rabbits hopping across a dewy meadow in bloom. I thought about waking right up and clipping Toenails where he stood and pushing his carcass into the hole with Joe, grabbing the widow by the hand, and running like two crazy fools in love. I took out a picture of Jeannie and the kids from my wallet. I looked, and looked, and looked at those smiling faces and white teeth and big titties on Jeannie, hoping against seemingly lengthening painful inevitable odds not to be joining Swinging Joe in Fresh Kills.

Read the Fine Print

And on the Seventh Day

◆ ◆ ◆

I'd killed six men in six days. And as much as I want to rest on the seventh, time is short. I have no choice but to get away from that Babylonian whore of a city. Boystown, Chicago. So now I'm in the 4Runner driving south and west. St. Louis is where I need to be next. I'm driving hard, faster than I should. There is a wicked shimmy in the fifteen-year-old steering column. Got to remember to adjust. Got to keep moving. I feel the demon's rank breath on the hairs of my neck. I have Pastor Dave's voice in my ear. He's telling me all sorts of things. All sorts of calming things, I tell you. Telling me to stay steady. Telling me to stay true. Telling me to let my faith steer me to my destination. I remove both hands from the steering wheel. Close my eyes. Feel the harsh, hot wind through the open windows. Feel the unmistakable acute rightward drift, fight opening my eyes, put but one finger back on the steering wheel, peek through narrow eyes, correct the drift, back to the black ribbon, moving fast, feeling a glorious spirit in and around me. It doesn't bother me a whit that God isn't talking to me just yet. I know He's busy with His work. If

He could talk to me at this moment, He would say *Keep moving, keep moving, you're close, almost there, keep moving.*

The six departed men were no good to anyone. Lowlife users and abusers. Low-wattage pleasure seekers. Sinners all. Low in the eyes of God. Lo and behold! God's wrath is upon you on this Judgment Day. The act of killing as an act of judgment and mercy is liberating. By the third one, I felt the rhythm one feels when breathing with purpose. An awareness of awareness, I'd say, like the father who carefully disciplines the child, just so, a firm hand with a gentle resolve to toughen morality. Morality ought to have a thick, coarse skin, said Pastor Dave. Beat it, prick it, bleed it, it heals and remains true. The thin-skinned morality bleeds out, withers, dies. I look at my hands gripping the wheel: thick and coarse. Hands that work.

The distant blue lights in the rearview mirror break the concentration. I look down. The needle vibrates past the 120 mark. I press harder on the pedal, will it through the floorboard, grip the wheel harder. And watch the reflection in the mirror make its gains.

I should slow down. Let him catch up. Pull over. Have him come on up. Take a measure of this character. See what needs to be seen. The hot air racing through the window smells divine. It smells of ploughed earth and freedom. I ease up on the pedal. Slow. It gets hotter. I smell manure as the wheels crunch along the shoulder. I stop. Put it in park. And I breathe.

The Past Making Good Time in Light Traffic

Testimony

◆ ◆ ◆

If your divorce court proceedings could possibly include a vignette along the lines of "I think the kids were down the street, at the Jarretts', but I can't remember exactly, and the live-in nanny was admiring my freshly bathed balls on the living room couch when my wife Patti came breezily through the open patio doors," then you've already set up shop in a place of trouble and grief. It's not that there was a nanny featured prominently in your tale of woe and surprise, *per se*. It could have been your wife's cousin Beth, a pro named Trixie; hell, it could have been your uncle Mort. The nanny part doesn't matter. It's that you were stupid enough to get caught. Anyway, you'll be getting to know the legal system intimately. And you'd better buy yourself an advanced abacus to keep you company as you plan and plot how you're going to screw her real good, make *her* live under a bridge, before she can screw you real good, make *you* live under a bridge.

That's how I thought of Jim Hurley's situation. Not that I would couch it in such terms, but there was no use in pretending it was anything other than what it was: the older rich white guy boning the young mocha-hued help. Yawn. There's no nuance here to catalogue and position. We'd seen it before. We'd see it again. Jim didn't seem particularly put out by the situation. He was going to have to spend some of that Oklahoma oil money of his to make it right. And right we'd make it. *Money's there to solve problems*, I tell my clients. We just need to limit and redefine the problems that need solving. Everyone was going to have to say some ugly things. Everyone was going to have to make some difficult decisions. Then everyone was going to walk away with some money.

Jim Hurley had other ideas.

"Okay. Here's how I'm looking at this thing. Patti and I killed someone, three years back, July fifth. A young Honduran girl. Illegal. Worked for us once or twice. She's out in San Diego East County. Someplace deep. I know where."

I nodded.

"It was a sex play thing. Rough housing. I have the video. Patti actually finished her off, but I'm in there. No use trying to pretend otherwise."

I nodded again.

"We buried her together."

"Okay."

"I want you to tell Rollins—in whatever legal way you see fit—I'm willing to burn myself and her 'cuz I'm not giving her the money I made while she sat around looking pretty and spending my money. No chance. I'll go as high as ten percent of total for her to piss off. That's our counteroffer."

"Jesus, Jim."

"Jerusalem Slim ain't got nothing to do with this."

"I agree."

"So, let's stay focused on the temporal."

I nodded.

"And the kids?"

"I'm responsible for the kids. They're off the table. If anything, I'm willing to give a bit on visitation."

I nodded again.

"Is this too much to ask you from a professional capacity?"

"I take it we're not discussing this in any other capacity."

"That's right."

"I'll call Rollins. Yes. Convey the proposal."

That was Tuesday morning.

Wednesday afternoon, I called Frank Rollins and relayed the proposal. I asked him to confer with his client and contact me at his convenience. He asked me if I could expound on the nature of the alleged crime committed by Mr. and Mrs. Hurley. I told him his client, of course, would be better positioned to share any related information. Frank Rollins said he'd get back to me. I closed the line. And went about other business.

The following Monday, after lunch, Frank Rollins called.

"Mrs. Hurley rejects Mr. Hurley's offer. Mr. Hurley is free to pursue any course of action he deems appropriate. Please advise as to Mr. Hurley's determination."

For the remainder of the week, I relayed messages back and forth. Mrs. Hurley wanted neither the five percent nor the ten percent Mr. Hurley offered. That she would not be pissing off without due process would be a fair conclusion. She would go for what the law said she ought to go for, or they both would fry. Not a problem.

I kept Jim apprised.

He came to see me the following week. He sat on my couch in complete and utter silence. And I mean he uttered not a sound of any kind. Like a Trappist monk, he sat in comfortable, unmoving repose looking at nothing in particular. I'm paid by the quarter hour, so I kept him company in silence. It was his time, so I didn't think, do, or pretend to think of anything else.

An hour and thirty-seven minutes later, he stood. "Take the video file to Lt. Hawkins. On the stick. Don't email it. I'll be at home."

"Do you want me to tell Rollins when we're giving up the video?"

"No."

I didn't want to say it, but I did. "Are you sure about this? We can give them one more chance. There's no coming back, Jim."

"Yes."

He picked up the document I'd prepared releasing me of my confidentiality. He took his time rereading it. Then he took out the pen from his breast pocket, uncapped it, and signed where indicated. He capped the pen, returned it, and walked out.

I booked his hour and a half, eating the final seven minutes, and thought of him off the clock. Pride? Revenge? Guilt? Atonement? Insanity? Somewhere along that sliding scale I could probably find his reason or reasons. You can never be certain about motivation beyond a reasonable doubt. Should I bother trying? Maybe some answers would make themselves obvious later, when regret made its entrance. I'd seen it happen before.

I could think back to when Jim got caught on the couch getting his junk worked on by the nanny as a quaint time. I could smile at the all-too-boring scenario of the old guy getting hot and bothered by the sweet young thing. We all of us have our crosses and *peccadillos* to bear. It could have been a short, silly, but expensive thing to get through. I was at a loss now for a funny scenario about where we would be going.

When Only the Best Will Do

Very *Not* Kosher

♦ ♦ ♦

I let the sack drop on the counter. Dusting off Brooklyn street dust and what-not from my coat. A job well done.

I said, "Got the kosher pork cutlets, instead. Cost a little more, organic sure, try 'em out first, then we can double the price on the high holidays, easy. That's what the man said."

Mamma Nussbaum looked into my smile. Flatly.

She said, "Who sold you kosher pork cutlets?"

I said, "New guy I found. Down Sixtieth. Bianchi, Biondi, something."

Mamma Nussbaum's short, powerful jab hit me square in the nose.

I stopped dusting. I cupped my nose. My tears welled. I could feel and taste my nose bleed.

I said, "What the fuck, Mamma?"

She looked like she might kill me right there. In the kitchen. With the knife she was clutching. She looked mad.

Mamma?

Boy Wondering

Las Palabras Bonitas del Amor

♦ ♦ ♦

I look at this boy, this son of mine, looking for signs of me, somewhere back in a time long ago, back before I could remember a thing. He's seven months old, a skinny little squirt, but sweet. Clear blue eyes. Pouty lips. Not much of a fusser at all. A bit like me with the blue eyes. Definitely the pouty lips of that deadbeat woman who pinched him out. I don't understand these women who up and leave these kids. Hell of a thing.

He's in his crib, asleep. I pick the food wrappers off the bare mattress, dropping them on the rug, kicking them out of sight. I look around the room for a blanket to cover him. I cover him with a green pillowcase, tucking the edge under his chin. I will be disappointing him in a few hours, and something drew me into the room. I would like for us to grow together, to do things together, to say things, to laugh, to share a beer in silence. Maybe we will. We have to have faith. I would like many, many things. I have a list. It's my little secret. And there are things on my list for my boy. He's snoring now, short nasal grunts. I touch his head and wispy brown hair. I wish he could remember these few minutes the way I'm starting to remember them. I wish I could say these things in a secret language only the two of us can understand. Like something deep in Spanish. No few minutes put together can ever mean anything much. He'll never know our few minutes here together, and that's sad. I'll always know, and that's sad, too. We'll go our different ways. He'll hold on to his sweetness for some time now. It's nice to think about the sweetness. And I can tell this one's got it in spades.

OK, baby. We'll both go our ways now. Your aunty'll take good care of you. Not a thing to worry about. That'll come later, the worrying, when you start putting things together and see they don't add up. I'll tell you this – then I'll go: it's how you make up the difference of the things that don't add up that makes all the difference. We work with what we're given. And you were given to me. I'll say to myself I'm doing this for you.

Keys to a Special Place No Longer Yours

A Real Sweetheart

◆ ◆ ◆

Yesterday, I sprayed piss and whatever diarrhea I could manage from an awkward stance on the bathroom stall floor and walls. It would give the bathroom cleaning crew something to do. Keep them busy. Make them wish they'd stayed in school. Make them see life is unfair. Object lessons, without a doubt.

Yeah, I'm *that* guy.

I'm frustrated. I've been without a home for thirty-six weeks. Without a job twice as long. I had long stopped regretting having been so difficult with my father and sisters. Some people are not made to be with one another.

I try to keep a low profile here in Union Station. A while back, I could hang around on the chairs in the waiting lounge. Take a load off. Ensconce my ass in plushy leather. Eat a little something. Take a nap. Read a book. Not anymore. They've changed the laws. Now I need to show a train ticket to enter the roped-off area. They've got Amtrak security guys in square caps that are paid to bust balls. They are happy in their work. I'm not going anywhere, so I don't have a ticket. I don't bother with those fools and their comfortable chairs anymore. And I'll be goddamned if I'm going to trek up the hill to the mission and hang around those hobos who are always looking around for something to take. They can all go to hell as far as I'm concerned. I was told there could be such a thing as dignity in poverty. I tried that route for a bit, but got angry with being poor.

I want to be free. I want to roam the earth like…you guessed it, Caine in *Kung Fu*. Hell, I'd go to China to become a kung fu master if I could. What I don't want is to have to earn money just to subsist. I want to live off the land, but not in an Alaskan wilderness kind of way. I'm not a Ted Kaczynski recluse. I want to be around people, but not as an unwashed bum. I can fish. I can hunt. I can cure meat. I can build things with my hands. I can scavenge. I can repurpose. I can get creative.

I tried walking out of this place. I headed out to Santa Monica and began walking north on the beach. I reeled in a good-sized halibut. I shared it with some RV types I came across digging a fire pit in the sand. They had wine, cheeses, and bread. It was a nice afternoon we spent together. I got as far as Malibu before getting arrested. They plucked me right out of the sand. They took my fucking hunting rifle. I had a permit for it once, but I haven't seen it in a long time. I spent a few nights in lockup. Then they kindly drove me back to the Los Angeles Mission. They gave me a bag lunch. I didn't even open it. I left it on the seat in the van. Nor did I thank them for the unasked-for bag of food or the unwanted ride. I walked down the little hill to Union. I can't stand being with those fucking bums for even a minute.

I still have my fishing pole. It gives me hope. I'm looking at my map. The coast is key. And there is a lot of coast in this country. I've been thinking of trying to walk south. Maybe try to get into Mexico. I speak about four words of Spanish, so that is going to be a problem. But getting through two hundred miles of English-speaking ball bustings to the border is going to be its own problem. I really should set up shop in Santa Monica. There are more options there. I'm torn, because here at Union there's always the off chance I can get a train ride to Louisiana or Florida or someplace. See their coasts. If I could get to the Texas coast, that might be interesting. I bet I could do what I want to do down in Galveston.

Today, I'm back in the bathroom. I wash up. They've done a nice job sprucing this place up. I feel like breaking something, like the paper towel dispenser. Or the soap dispenser. But I need those things. But I also need a better plan. And there are no better plans in here. Nor out there. Nor if I walked a mile or ten. Nor if I could reach the coast and walk the shores forever. Maybe I'll walk out into the ocean itself and keep walking until the bottom gives way, then I can float to wherever the current takes me that day.

Naughty Rooster Nobody Can Catch

capture, but now a specialist is on his t...

se.
udy, in particu-
s causing a flap
ttsburgh, and
no one has
ble to catch
The home-
ailed. A city
r failed.
-control
ailed. An
ity solici-

Rudy

belonging
Gaston,
belong
ton. He
and
roost
squa
yard
ran
hi
t

Now, it's up to Mr.
St. Louis, a school
ficer who appre-
ens in his spare

lives on property

The other
slower, w
animal-c
cated to
stops b
P

More Famous Than You

Cock Teasing

◆ ◆ ◆

I fucking hate chickens. Roosters in particular. That strutting through shit like they're the cock of the walk makes me piss blood. They remind me of my cousin. And I hate my cousin. Given my druthers, I would much rather work at a place like Perdue's. Killing chickens day in and day out would put my mind in a better place. I've got to bide my time in this work-release program hellhole for the time being. Shoveling animal shit from here to there is not my idea of anything, especially when I can squint across the fields and see all these fucking chickens running around free and organic in their very own enclosure, free from fear and free from want. It's not right for a fucking chicken to be closer to Roosevelt's American dream than me.

But it all pooled into a moot puddle when six federal marshals rolled up in three cars on Tuesday, fanned out, and started walking toward me. I leaned on my shovel watching this impressive Wyatt Earp-meets-the-Untouchables display of shotgun-toting, Kevlar-wearing American machismo. They closed in fast, forming a semi-circle around me and my shovel.

I looked at the one clearly running the show. "Golly, Sheriff. What gives?"

"Bill Estes, you're under arrest for the murder of Hugh Estes. They got you dead to rights, son. Hands behind your back."

I complied. Miranda sang sweet nothings in my ear as they placed the cool steel on my hot, wet wrists. Then I was prodded forward. We walked in silence at a leisurely pace toward where the chickens ruled the world. What a nice place these fucking chickens had—nice little picket fence, tall grass, wild flowers, a coop that looked like a giant Swiss cottage, and the sky above them a deep, beautiful blue. I bet they wished they could fly.

The cars were parked to the side of the chicken château. I was eased into the backseat. The door closed. I looked out the spotless window at the chickens. And wouldn't you know it. There was this one little rooster fucker staring at me through the bars in the fence. We locked eyes, and I willed him dead. The car pulled forward. I wrenched my neck trying to keep my stare intact for a moment longer. The moment passed. As I stared ahead, I thought if that little chicken fucker also wished for my death, he'd win. Fucking chicken. I don't want to live anymore, anyway. Sticking that chickenshit turd Hugh could be spun six ways to life without parole. No. I'd fess up to the other three I throttled and this little road trip here just starting would have a terminal stop at potassium chlorideville.

Someone's Coming

Transactions

◆ ◆ ◆

I am the water. Happiest when at the mercy of gravity's pull, flowing along paths of least resistance. Saddest when pooled, stagnant, evaporating. Tonight, gravity is pulling me toward you in your house in Boyle Heights. You've been plugged into the GPS, and I'm flowing to you at high rates of speed. The contract stipulates you gunned before midnight. I don't know why. Nor why the wait for the last possible moment. I don't ask questions I can't answer myself. There's a $25,000 incentive bonus that expires at midnight. I'm incentivized. It is 10:42 now. I will have you dead, pictured, and texted with time to spare. Don't worry.

At 11:11 I am at your Craftsman. There's a Passat behind the Camaro in the driveway. The hoods are cold to the touch. I'll assume there's a woman in there with you. I let my imagination flicker in picturing what you two have been up to in there. Maybe I'll see me a pair of live titties tonight. I'll consider it a perk.

The living room lights are on. The curtains are drawn. There is no sidewalk traffic. No nosey neighbors.

I knock on the kitchen door off the driveway. You answer the door without even asking who it is, pushing it outward, and die like a whisper. I surge forward like water breaching your sand castle, close the door, step over you, and through the dining room into the living room.

Where is she?

There she is. In her plush fabric La-Z Boy nest, in shorty-shorts and a pink wife-beater, looking overheated, with oddly puffy feet at, what, the home stretch of the third trimester? Reclined there like an anaconda on a river bank after a meal of unhappy capybaras. Asleep.

For fuck's sake.

I holster the piece. I admire her smooth, shiny, glistening skin and rhythmic breathing for long moments. Then a few moments more.

I turn back to the kitchen. A colorful, spreading mess. One picture. Two pictures. Three pictures. No doubts. All sent at 11:25.

The screen reads *Delivered*.

I wait.

Then it reads *Read*.

I'll go see the man now about getting paid.

On Hold

Father & Daughter

◆ ◆ ◆

I hear she found some trouble. Or trouble found her. No one told me which. All they said she's up Vegas some ways. The closest I ever came to being with her was the afternoon I was squirting a sackful of sixty-Kools-a-day mentholated jizz into her momma. Right before her step-daddy pried me off her, hauled me to the stationhouse, and had me sent here for my third-and-out statutory pop. He was a fine one to be making judgments and ratting people out, let me tell you. And as that dirty old buzzard was peeling me off her, I remember thinking, "That one felt like the one that gets her." I had strong feelings for that girl. Still probably do. She grew up nice from the pictures I've seen. And now that our little girl has found herself some trouble, I feel troubled myself. Like I've done her wrong. Like I should'a done better. Funny thing is, if I'd done the right thing and kept off her fifteen-year-old momma that one last time, she wouldn't have come along. Wouldn't have found trouble. Wouldn't have been troubled. I wouldn'a be here. Wouldn'a be thinking about how I'd done her wrong 'cuz I'd done right to begin with. But I'd have no daughter to be proud of me for having done right. A man needs kin. Needs to feel connected. Needs to have pride. And this business with her troubles is making me rethink the life I no longer have.

And that's sad.

They're letting me make a phone call. Free of charge, as always. I been real good in here. No trouble. I'm just minding my business like I'm minding my time. Two years to go. I dial a number. After two rings, Roger answers.

"Roger, it's me. Donny."

"Donny! How you been, boy?"

"Can't complain. Hey, what's this I hear about Melinda? Trouble of some sort."

"Yeah, well. You know."

"I don't."

"Knifed some young guy in Vegas. Cheated her on a deal, or something like that."

"What kind of deal?"

"Hell if I know. I been keeping my beak clean these days. I don't even *think* of bad shit any more. These days."

"I'm trya get a hold of her."

"What for, now? You ever even talk to her before?"

"No–"

"So, what you want to talk to her for?"

"Maybe I can help her with her troubles."

"Nah. She don't need your help. She up in Johnson Correctional. Took a plea. Boy didn't die. She'll be out in a few years. Easy time, Johnson."

"Well, shit."

"Hey, you see Feely, tell him that piece of land he's been yakking about got bought. Last Thursday."

"Yeah, sure. Hey, can you get me the number to call her up there?"

"Who?"

"Melinda."

"What for?"

"I wanna see if I can help."

"I guess. Does she even know your name?"

"Yeah. Sure she does. Her momma told her."

"Marla took off with Ben Vincent about a month ago. Went to Florida."

"Sure. I know Ben. Good for them."

"I like Ben."

"Knifed a guy, huh?"

"Yeah. In the leg or something."

"Poor kid."

I fell to thinking about that knife.

"Listen, Donny. I gotta go. Call me next month."

He hung up. I held the phone to my cheek a while, trying to think of what to say when I called her. I tried to imagine her on the other end of the line. Tried to imagine what my voice might sound like to her. I wanted her to know I could be there for her.

"Hey Melinda-girl, it's Daddy," I said.

That sounded real good. Real natural. I'd have time to practice it more.

A Place to Have Thoughts

Of Two Minds

◆ ◆ ◆

I stood there a solitary man of two minds. A gun in my hand weighed the same. But something in my older mind and not in my younger man's one would have shot him if the older one was thinking of what the younger one had passed on to him.

And that's the difference between the free older man and the incarcerated younger one.

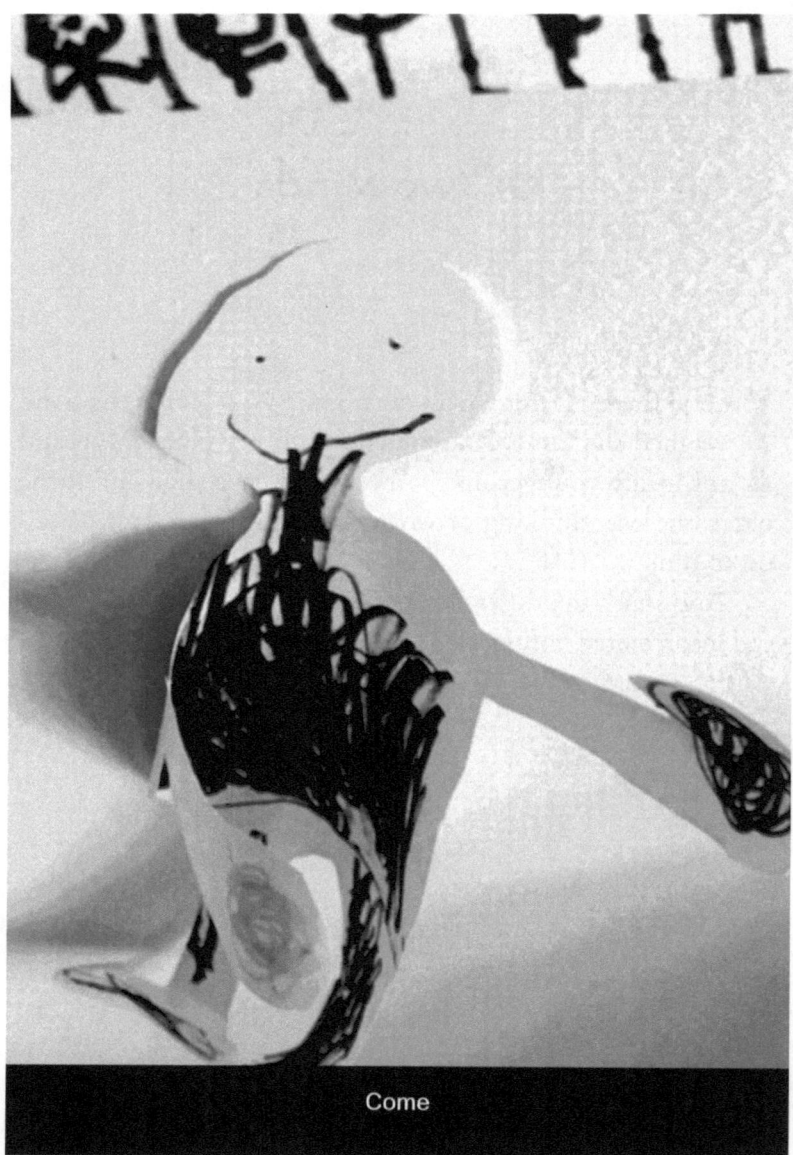

Come

Gases and Guesses

◆ ◆ ◆

Look at this video. Here, let me click it.

Now, look at it. Look.

Those are Syrian six-year-olds. A whole classroom of them. Choking to death on sarin gas. Or chlorine. I don't really know.

Don't turn. Just keep watching.

There's nothing anyone can do for them. Look at those adults in a panic. Look at those poor children. You're lucky I have this thing on mute. The sounds are horrible. They're choking to death. Their lungs are on fire. You just want to go in there and do something. Their lungs are dying.

No. Hold on. Wait, wait.

It takes a long time to die from this stuff, but mercifully the video is short.

Wait.

Not much longer.

[silence]

You're going to tell me anyone can watch this, then have the magical fairy balls to tell me there is a just and merciful god anywhere in the universe?

[silence]

Not much longer now. Stay with me.

You know who's not much better? That fuck Nietzsche. He killed any hope we could have for a decent god by saying he's already dead inside of us. Said we killed him ourselves. Guess it made men mad. Or crazy. And hateful. Look at this. Gave us the first war and mustard gas and chlorine gas. What a pisser. Haven't looked back since.

You still watching?

Yea, once you cross a certain point, there's no looking away. That's why we'll always have it.

Long Day Ahead

The Little Things

◆ ◆ ◆

I'm not much of much. I don't think so anymore, anyway. I
used to think I was much. But that was a while ago. I played
on the Internets. I met older men. I showed them my titties
every now and again. We'd meet up, sometimes. They'd buy
me things. Maybe a crystal Swarovski forget-me-not. Maybe
dinner at Red Lobster. Maybe a weekend trip to Savannah.
I liked being someone's idea of a dream. I was always in the
right. No need to argue. The older guys are like that. They like
when I show them things on the phone. Calms them down.
Gets them going. It depends. I could get married. At any time.
I've had the offers. I've schemed with the married ones. But
it's only with the soul mates that I take any of this stuff seri-
ously. Like Brian. And I'm Brianne. Cute. Almost like fate.
Like a conspiracy or plot of some sort, is what Brian had said.
B&B. Bed & Breakfast. BB guns. We had two T-shirts made.
Two B's in a Pod. I saw his wife once while wearing mine. It
was funny, I thought. She didn't know me. She had no clue. I
know all about her. Brian said she didn't pay too close attention to details. I wasn't much worried about her, anyway. She

was old. She looked old. She dressed old. And about his son, Taylor, I may have asked once. Or twice. It would be strange to start something new with something from the old. I felt my mind changing. Felt like I deserved all new things. I may have told Brian this one time. Or two times. We didn't really talk about it too much. I didn't want to quit him. Not right away. But I could, if I had to. But then Brian did the strangest of things. He left that boy of his in the car for a whole day. An entire July Atlanta day. Out in the open sun, no garage or anything like that. It got to something like 105 degrees outside. Something like 120 degrees inside the car. Or more. That's what the news was saying afterwards. I can't imagine. That boy died before the morning was through. The news said Brian checked on the car a few times during the day. I remembered I showed him my titties over the phone on his lunch break that very day. Noon, I think. He was in his cubicle. Eating a sandwich. He seemed happy to see them. Not like someone who knew his boy was broiling in a car.

I told the police, then the jury, all this. I was very honest.

I never want to see that Brian again.

I shouldn't have done what I done. I know it's easy to tempt a man. And with a married one, it makes me a sinner. Every time I get into a hot car, I close my eyes and hate what I maybe helped do a little bit more. I don't put the air conditioning on for a long time. It's like Christ warning me not to be a bad girl anymore. Telling me, "Here's what sin feels like, B." He's with me inside those hot cars. And I feel blessed. Saved.

Scene of the Crime

Help

◆ ◆ ◆

It's heartbreak. When you read about it. When you try to imagine it happening. A young woman out for a constitutional with her father is gunned down. On the Embarcadero in San Francisco. Mid-afternoon. Early July. A place alive with people. Single bullet to where the heart and lungs are busy with the day's business of living. Her father is on the ground with her. In a frenzy. Floating on instincts. And the penultimate thing she has left to do in her conscious life is say:

"Dad, help me. Help me, Dad." There are no sadder, more devastating words imaginable. People are crying. Helpless.

At this point, one wants to look north, to look away, to follow the man with a gun and bloodless heartlessness walk away. He's not insane. His senses of self-preservation and liberty are taking him away from the scene deliberately, head down, looking at feet that take him away. He will be seen and heard from again. He will soon enough become a bit of a data point in the bit part every participant in rituals of violence plays on the altar of the 2nd Amendment.

And the young woman, too. In her due time. She'll play her American role. She needs to die first. And she's actively doing so, despite her pleas, despite her father's frenzies, despite the suspended gasp and solemn murmurings of a random audience, despite the ambulance and police and fire sirens that echo as if off the hills and the surface of the bay's calm July waters ... so calm and chilled and surprisingly fragrant ... Fucking guns!

"Dad?" Her ultimate verdict on life is surprise. [She is surprised.] Her father is surprised. The uniformed men and women pushing through the crowd have seen this before, have done this before. No surprises as they get to work. Stabilizing. OK. OK. This is the best we're going to get on this sidewalk. Lift. Push. The crowd parts. The daughter is silent, as if resting. The father follows the daughter.

She dies two hours later. Unhelped.

The man who shot her is arrested three hours later. No resistance. He is cuffed and gently eased into the squad car.

The rest you imagine.

Still Together

Myths

◆ ◆ ◆

My father's a myth now. No longer real. He's what I need him to be. He's an ideal toward which others can only aspire. He's what they think was said of Lincoln, belonging now to the ages—the ages of my time horizon, at least.

He's my myth now. He's who I think I see moving through a crowd. He's like hope no longer hope, having almost come to fulfillment only to … fade away. He's whom I appeal to when I close my eyes, asking for help, expecting wisdom and reassurance. He's the distant past, where once he'd been the very cord tethering me to the distant past. I want to ask the right questions. He has so many answers.

I had a dream which I wrote down to remember. I am on the balcony of our apartment in Beirut. I am smoking a cigarette. It burns in the ashtray. He walks out on to the balcony. I stand abruptly. "It's you," I say, stepping toward him, but my real thoughts are of shame. I don't want him to know I've started smoking again.

I tried hard not to disappoint him while he lived.

The myth is what's gained when the man is lost. And like the man gone, the myth needs tending to: rituals, memorials, celebrations. The myth stays alive so long as I can keep the need for the myth alive. Someday it will cease being anything at all. And the both of us will only be found in the dust that contains us.

The day is here. The moment is now. I'm standing on the dirt that will soon contain me. They won't bother to move me too far from the place they fell me. I've come a long way to be here. My imagination has travelled even farther. I'd thought these Islamic State fuckers the same as Nazis. Nothing from the well-thumbed book of depravity was going to shock me with this crew. Still doesn't. I felt the role of righteous exterminator, truly the great mercenary infidel they've labeled me. I'd killed four, maybe five in a running battle through the olive fields outside Idlib. My conscience is as clear as an alpine lake, even after the concussion of the mortar round knocked me senseless, rendered me helpless. Now I am captured. I lost and this is my consequence.

I'm far, far afield now. I'd wanted my last thoughts to be of my father. I have no son, so the both of us will end here. It's spring in the desert and still the blade is cold against my throat. Fear makes everything seem cold. I'd felt it before. I'm alone fighting this... barbaric evi-

Dreams

GiGi Got Rolled

◆ ◆ ◆

He was going to roll that old man. Roll that old Italian man with a little girl's name. Roll him if it were the very last thing he ever did. He'd had it. Had it up to here. No self-respecting young man could live forever on the whim of someone else's largess. It could only humor him so far. And this was far enough.

Caitlin strolled out of the bathroom, her towel a tight mauve beehive teetering on her head. She hummed a tune. *Bewitched*. But she thought it was *I Dream of Jeannie*. Nick-at-Night played on the television. Roy lay on the bed, head on stacked pillows, eyes closed, thinking of things. Caitlin stood at the mirror, poking her naked self.

From the bed: "You turn that water off?'

The humming stopped. "Mmm hmmm." Annoyance. Derision. A tired routine.

"I hear dripping."

Major Tony did something stupid. Jeannie blinked him away. Arctic exile. The Major shivered and stewed, the laugh track queued.

"It does that. Then it stops." She touched herself again.

Roy listened to the dripping. They'd been to Lake Mead. They'd seen the plunging waterline. Los Angeles had no business letting its faucets drip. He listened. It dripped. He reached for the remote and muted the shrill commercial.

"It's still dripping."

The girl turned from the mirror and strode back into the bathroom. The nylon curtain ripped back under metal clanging. The dripping stopped. Roy closed his eyes. When he opened them again, the girl was back at the mirror. Jeannie had already blinked the Major back to the house. It had been another silly misunderstanding.

"I've got an idea," Roy said.

Caitlin was poking at her thigh.

"Mmm hmmm."

"What say you and me take GiGi's car, some money, and just get out of here?"

Caitlin stopped poking herself. "Take his car as in borrow it?"

"Take his car as in ours to keep. You know I've had my eye on that thing for like forever. A cherry red American boy's wet dream."

"You're a stupid little boy. You know that? You're so stupid I won't even say anything else. I mean, why would you do that to someone who's been so nice to you? And to me, too."

"What's so nice about making me feel like a worthless shitbird?"

"I have no idea what you're blubbering about."

"Don't you think I can have some self-respect? Do you think it feels good to be felt sorry for? Why else you think GiGi give us this nice place to stay in and money and food when we're a little hard up? He feels sorry for us. He thinks we're losers with nowhere to go."

"Oh, poor baby. Lounging around in someone else's guest house FOR FREE and doing part-time work when the mood strikes is just so terrible. Oh boo the fuck hoo. How lucky can we possibly get? Our own little cottage? A nice yard? A really nice old man who trusts us with everything he's got? He just wants a little company. How stupid and selfish can you be?"

Roy was silent for a moment. "I don't trust people who are so fucking nice and generous. It gives me the creeps."

"Leave. Get up and go."

"That's what I'm saying. Let's get out of here once and for all."

"I'm starting to feel real stupid just even knowing you."

"You know what our problem is, you and me?"

The girl shrugged.

"We lack ambition. We don't have a goddamn thing going for us."

Caitlin looked at the silent television and admired Jeannie's bustiness.

"So, what else is new?"

"It's time we made some new, that's what's new."

"And stealing GiGi's car is making something new?"

"Yes. And he won't even call the police. He's that nice!"

"Let's just ask him, then."

"No! I'm tired of that old man giving me things. I'm taking things this time."

"You have no idea how stupid you sound."

Roy sat up. "I'm ready right now. Right now. No suitcase. No toothbrush. No planning. No nothing. No one's going to call me a layabout ever again. You coming?"

Caitlin looked down at her naked body. "I don't have a thing to wear."

Roy was off the bed and digging through the top drawer of the bureau. He pulled out a stack of bills held together by a rubber band.

"Oh shit. Really? His money, now? You're going to steal from one of the nicest people on the planet?"

With his other hand, Roy pulled up two keys on a loop. He clanged them together. "Twice."

"You're an idiot and an ungrateful jackass."

"Say what you will. But I've got twenty thousand dollars in cash and a mint old Chevelle. Only got twenty-five thousand miles on it. That fool never went anywhere."

Roy moved toward the door. "Last chance."

"So stupid."

"We'll see." He was out the door.

Caitlin sat on the bed. She turned off the television. Outside, the old car roared to life and rolled down the driveway. She heard it accelerate down the street. She slid her phone off the nightstand, unlocked it, and tapped 9-1-1.

Following

Jessie

◆ ◆ ◆

He was getting into a comfortable tea-bagging squat when the phone started vibrating along the nightstand top. I swatted at those musty, fleshy, Reagan-era knick-knacks dangling at my nose. He rolled off to his right, grasping, squealing invectives. I rolled to my right, reaching for the phone.

"Jessie. He's home now." It was my mother.

"How's he look?"

"Not so good. Not so terribly good."

I sat up.

"Okay."

One of us closed off the line.

I stood and moved to the chair for my underwear and dress. I slipped into the sandals. I opened my purse and took out the $400. I peeled off ten twenties. I returned to the nightstand and propped the remaining bills against the lamp.

"I'm taking two for having gotten so close to those things."

He was still clutching his affronted bibelots. "That really hurt, Jess."

"Yeah, well, you need to work on your quickness."

I rubbed a finger along his cheek as I walk by the bed.

"Your dad?"

"Yeah."

I was at the door.

"When will I see you again?"

"Call me in a few weeks."

I opened the door and walked out.

It's almost obligatory to think something about Vegas as you drive around any of its straight-as-an-arrow streets. Vegas is a weird sensation. Let's all meet out in the desert for two, three days and do stuff with or to one another that would never fly anywhere else. That's the cachet, at least, the multi-billion-dollar, multi-year, multi-entendre branding campaign. Aside from that base marketing logic, there's no reason for Las Vegas to exist. Like all vanity, it needs facelifts and more than a modicum of the suspension of disbelief to believe in itself. I believe in it because it's home. I know it well. It's hot. It's thirsty. It's not the kind of place you'd want to find yourself lost in. You either come here with someone, or you shouldn't come here at all.

My mother was at the door when I pushed it open. She looked like the old whore she was. Worn, droopy, gaudy dress, indifferent to your thoughts of her. A cigarette smoked between her fingers. I kissed her through the smoke on the tip of her nose.

"He's upstairs."

I climbed the stairs to where my father would be.

I stood in the doorway and smiled at him. A large man in scrubs sat in a chair at the end of the bed. We nodded to one another.

"I could step out if you'd like."

"That would be nice. Thank you."

He stood and left.

I moved the chair to my father's side and sat. I took his hand. It was cool and smooth. He looked thin, weak, younger somehow, but clean, like he was spruced up for something big.

"Well, look at you. You got out one last time. Not a lawman in sight to hold you to this bed. You were right, I'll give you that. Born free, dying free. I hear you saying it. But we all know it was all that time going in and getting out that got you going. How many times did you say it to me? Serious and joking. A hundred? Five hundred? Should I say it aloud one more time, just between the two of us? Listen, I'll whisper it: There is no sin. There is the perception of sin. There is, though, desire. That is real enough. We understood desire, didn't we? Got us a lot of nice things. I'm going to miss you, Dad. Miss you and miss you. But no soapy horseshit nonsense, right? Not now. Not here. You got it. This one last time. I'll say what you would say: He was alive when I left him, Your Honor."

I took out my phone and swiped to the tape-recording app. I pressed play. I pressed the speaker button. I placed the phone on the pillow near his head. There was the whirring beats of a ceiling fan. We had been in Casa Grande

Transitional, courtesy of the State of Nevada Department of Corrections. Then my father cleared his throat. I remembered how he looked.

"Where were you before you were born?"

"I don't know. Nowhere."

"Nowhere before. Nowhere after. And we don't know the goddamned difference. We're born. We live. We die, Boo Boo. That's just how it is."

"I know."

"I came to know I missed you something real fierce before you were born. Maybe you'll do the same after I'm gone. If I played 'em right."

"You played them just right."

"Well, there you go. Good. Turn that fucking thing off."

Then nothing more.

It felt good to smile. I picked up the phone and tucked it into my purse. I took his chin in my hand and kissed the tip of his nose. And walked out. And never looked back. And felt happy, happy with the things he'd taught me, the memories we'd made, and the things we'd laughed at. The stuff of missing.

Someone Up There Likes Me

Weaknesses

◆ ◆ ◆

I have a weakness for redheads and cigarettes. And booze. She couldn't know how sweet a setup it looked to me, of course, as she leaned against the wall on the sidewalk outside Pete & Shorty's, dragging hard on a thin white stick. The street lamp bathed her in glowing white like an angel of the Lord. I ignored the tavern door, my thirst a razor-sharp edge, and walked up to her instead.

"Hey, Red. Spare one?"

She held out her pack and shook a few upward. I took one. Put it to my lips. The tip was wet. Soaked. I tried to think of something to explain this. I didn't want to press it, but I couldn't let it go, either.

"It's not every day you get a moist filter fresh outta the box," I said. I flicked the Zippo open and snapped a flame to life.

"You dissatisfied, put it back in here." She held out the open box with a steady hand.

"Too late now, Red," I said, showing her the lit smoke between my fingers. I snapped the Zippo shut.

"I'm happy for you."

I was glad she was happy, as I was getting happy, too.

We two happy people stood on the sidewalk in silence and smoked.

After a while: "You from around here?"

She pointed her cigarette to the second or third floor of the brownstone directly across the street.

Well, shit!

"Funny. Been coming to Pete's for years now. Never seen you before."

"First time coming inside, tonight."

I studied the borrowed cigarette trance-like—"It's like magical fate."—and beamed widely.

"No. It's not. I used to go to Zonka's. And now I'm trying this place."

I looked back over my shoulder down the sidewalk to the small smoking crowd fidgeting outside Zonka's.

"Got tired of the Zonk crowd?"

"You're a nosey peckerwood."

I raised my hand to show her the prison ink above my thumb. "Nothing gets by you, does it?"

"You mustn't have been in there too long. No one this nosey lasts very long."

"Just making pleasant conversation. How about that Zonk crowd?"

"They had their moments."

"Those moments got too much for you, huh?"

"I stuck someone. Stuck him for being a horny ass."

"Well, now … That's a conversation starter. What did the law have to say about that?"

"Sure, they took me in. They came right to the bar and took me off my stool. I didn't hide a thing. I told them every possible detail they could want to hear. I gave them the blade."

"No PD or anything, huh?"

"For what? So stupid. I know as much about what the cops want to hear as any of those limpnics."

"True. Sad, but true. Then?"

"Then, what? Like two hours later, I hear Metzler in the ER tells them pretty much the same thing I told them. Which is lucky for him. I would've been pretty pissed if he tried to stick this one on me. Pretty pissed."

"Yes. I can believe this."

"They told him to keep his hands to himself and his swizzle stick zipped up. End."

"Well, that was lucky for everyone all around."

She dropped her smoke to the sidewalk near the ashtray and snuffed it with rhythmic vigor under the toe of her sandal. "They told us not to come back. Apparently, they don't condone that kind of behavior. So, I'm stuck coming to this shit hole."

She yanked the door open and went inside.

I took my time finishing my smoke, looking up into the night, counting star specks, counting far-away possibilities.

Escape Plan B

Slim Pickings

◆ ◆ ◆

Another frustrating night at Joey's. Just more of the same ball-busting nonsense that had long settled over me like fine dust. Drink. Shoot the shit. Shoot rounds of pool. Throw a dart or two. Take Marcy after closing time to the car parked out back. Let my mind wander as she bobs her head in my lap like a chicken. Probably angling for a deep dicking. Man, in this town—slim pickings.

Justin, the renegade country singer. If only I could strum a guitar.

The rhythms of this place are driving me to distractions. I'm not sure why leaving this sad sack of a town doesn't seem like a viable option. It's not so much finding something aside from roofing to do as it is what else can I think of. It's not boredom or laziness. Conroe is home, sure. Everyone is here. Everything tomorrow will be like yesterday. We say we like it that way. But how can that be any different than in any other place? You hear about guys who took off out of town to take a chance. There is envy there, sure. The great big unknown. A great adventure. A new place with new people doing new things. More girls. Better jobs. More money. But who knows? Failing in a bigger place would feel bigger. I mean, failing in New York or Los Angeles would feel like the definitive end to a journey, the dead end of the adventure. And when tomorrow starts to feel like yesterday every day, where do you go to start again from those kinds of places?

Here, I can go to a place like Joey's, get drunk, goof around, get blown, then drive off the buzz and sleepiness, drive out in the emptiness and darkness like it would have been had we not invented ambition. I did exactly that on Monday. And as soon as Marcy's done, I'll do it again tonight.

A Room for Rest

Commandments

◆ ◆ ◆

It had been seven days since I'd violated the Tenth Commandment doggy style. Ed Bilbao was downstairs, calling out to me, rapping his knuckles against the screen door frame. It was a few minutes before eleven. I had a nice gin buzz going. I was in one of my why-the-fuck-not moments. I went down the stairs, calling out, "Ed, it's open. Come on in." By the time I reached the foot of the stairs, Ed was in the foyer with wandering eyes and a guilty posture.

"Looking to get a quick night-time nine innings," I said, pointing at the nasty-looking mahogany bat slapping against his calf.

"I got grievances, Bob."

"Looks maybe you've put a few back tonight, Ed."

"We need to talk, Bob. I got grievances."

"Sure, let's get down to brass tacks. Why not leave that thing outside?"

Ed looked down at his slugger. "It's part of my grievances."

"Sure. Let's go into the kitchen."

Ed shuffled after me down the short hallway to the kitchen dimly lit by a stove light. By the time he crossed on to the linoleum, I brought my own bat, this one of the aluminum softball variety, savagely across the front of his skull. As he dropped, I swung again, glancing the side of his head from the opposite direction.

I didn't hear the crack of the hits or the crumpled thump of the fall or anything else because the inside of my head was ringing with angry gin, fear, and adrenaline.

I put the bat back in the wall rack and stepped around Ed to the phone charging on the counter.

I dialed 9-1-1.

"What's the nature of my emergency? Jesus God! I have a mess on my kitchen floor. My neighbor Ed Bilbao came at me with a baseball bat. But I got him first."

I listened.

"I don't know any of that CPR stuff. He looks dead to me. And I'm not touching him. No idea what to do."

The 9-1-1 man said some other stuff. Then I gave him my address.

I sat down on a stool.

I saw Ed's wallet resting against the far wall. I tried to imagine how it had been pried from his pocket. Was he holding it in his hand? I went over to it and picked it up. I took out three twenties and left one ten and three ones.

I wondered if they'd fingerprint it. I dropped it back on the floor anyway.

I was back on the stool when I heard the sirens. I was breathing calmly. I was trying to remember what Jill's body looked like. We'd both been drunk. We did it in their backyard against the picnic table. She hadn't been worth it. Not by a long shot. And Ed would probably say the same thing. I wondered what prison smelled like. I wondered what prison food tasted like.

I heard the screen door open. "Police."

"In here. The kitchen. Down the hall."

Ed Bilbao moved his arm slowly along the floor.

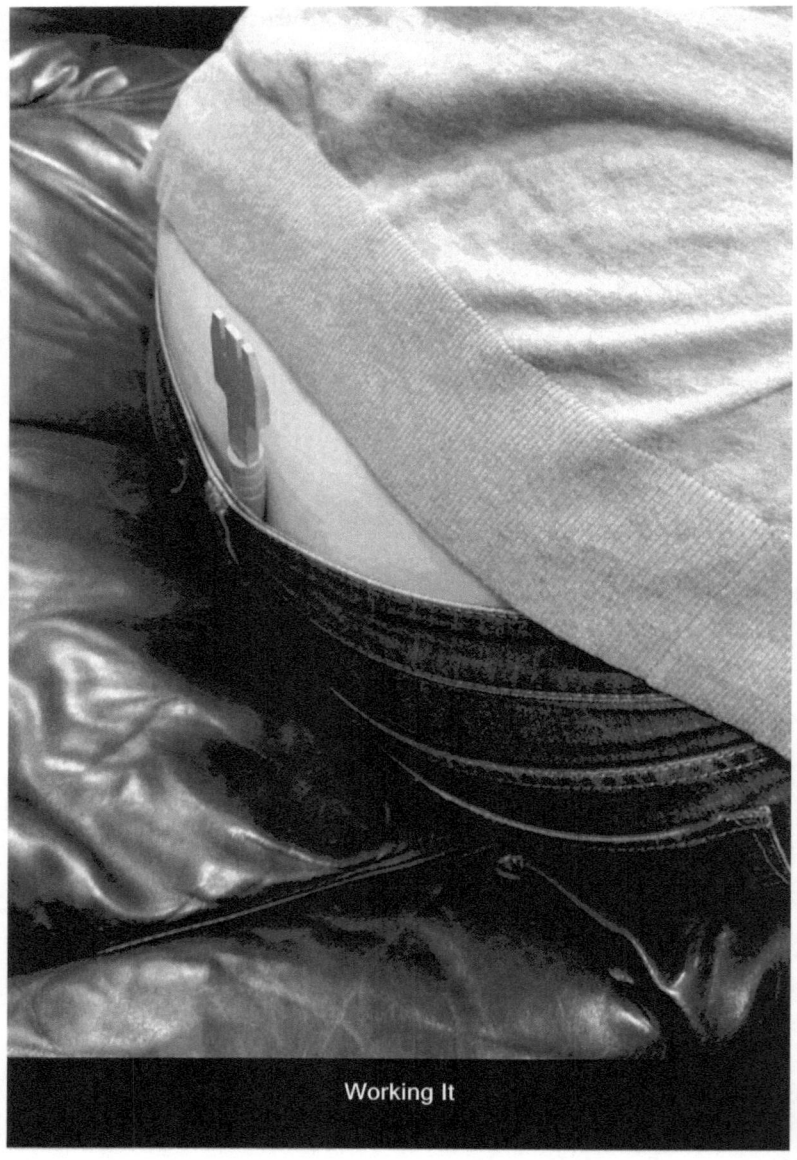

Working It

Ms. Fanny Mae Lubrano

◆ ◆ ◆

I t's good to get off my feet for a little bit.

I'm the luckiest girl alive and here I am, poolside—my pool—overlooking a blue Pacific on one of those California days meant for doing nada thing at all. The phone is upstairs. Theresa is off in Santa Cruz watching her son graduate. The gates are locked. I've made myself a grilled ahi tuna steak and mushroom salad for lunch. I'm 27 years old and have assets in the neighborhood of $842 million. Not a penny inherited. Sort of.

It's a simple story.

I have an ass that's been described as the Sophia Loren of asses. I wouldn't make this up. An Italian daily—*la Repubblica*—wrote a paean (roughly translated) to "this glorious outcropping that reminds one of a more innocent, caring, fecund time when lust could be the virtue upon which men dedicated themselves toward more harmonious relations with their immortal soul. If not God, perhaps this perfect, faultless thing." *Che figata*! Do I have this article reproduced and framed in my guest cabana bathroom? Yes, I do. If you can read Italian, you're in for a treat of some over-the-top man-prose from a much-imitated era that has permanently stained the imagination of my male contemporaries.

So, what does it all mean?

In the grand scheme of things, not a thing. I don't have the novelty or all-around ooh-la-la-ness of a Monroe. That, and I'm hoping to make it (well) past my fortieth birthday. So far so good. I tend to it with the same care I tend to any other part of me. Decent diet. Some exercise. Absolutely NO foreign funny things in any form. When it balloons and starts to sag, so be it. I've had a good run.

I won't denigrate American culture as degenerate because I make nearly as much money on all continents, save maybe from the penguins and researchers in Antarctica. I wear other people's skirts, dresses, jeans, underwear, swimwear, short shorts, shoes, leggings, long sweaters. My anime ass graces bento boxes for businessmen in Japan. I've got a fragrance from Chanel. I'm featured in urban pimp-ho video games, a booty call app, a YouTube channel with 38 million followers. To see some ass jiggling, you've got to first watch an ad. Coke. Nike. Apple. Wells Fargo. Macy's. Kanye (of all people!) put out a raunchy ditty "Fanny's Fanny," some tiny speck of a country in the South Pacific wanted to put a tanned version of it on a stamp. I passed on that one. They used it instead for a tourist campaign. My venture fund invests in fashion technologies (yes, there is such a thing). I give out scholarships. I could go on and on. It's cash inflow all day, every day. You want to maximize returns on diversified assets, you come talk to me. Alas, there will be no IPO.

I'm told I'm filling a need. I'll buy that. We're creatures of appetites. That's probably the easiest way for me to get and keep a grip on things. Simplicity, right? It's more than the actual consuming of things. It's also about the availability of things. It's also about things that stimulate other things. Because it's simply inconceivable to be making so much money, to be the object of so much attention, to be deferred to as a morally superior woman solely based on two heavenly spheres of God-molded fat and muscle. Should I even bother telling you what happened when a gust of wind on Majorca blew my skirt up and the cameras were rolling and … well, you guess the rest. On the surface of it, it makes no sense. You've got to dig deeper. You've got to try to get into the head of the person who is shelling out the money. I don't pass judgment on the person doing all the shelling, even though sometimes I feel sad. Sad because the logical conclusion to reach is that access to my ass is a gateway to something else. What that something else is or may be is probably best left to the imagination. We grab our kicks and inspirations any way we can get them. No judgments, right?

This is all no sweat off my back. I don't find it particularly stressful doing what I do. Someday, though, I will try to walk away from it. After I reach a billion. I will take my toys and my treasures and go someplace hard and expensive to get to. Malta. Sardinia. Fiji. I have no idea. But I suspect fame to be what Faulkner said about the past: You may be done with it, but it's not done with you. If that proves to be the case, then no matter where I am, I'll be back to where I am now—working appetites and gateways for money. Maybe I'll get married.

Maybe I'll have children. Maybe they'll run the enterprises when everything is starting to come back down to earth. But no matter what, I know I'm a lucky girl. I take nothing for granted. And I am grateful for a great many things and people. My kooky parents gave me a funny-ass name that's long been trademarked, but they also gave me their genes. They know how grateful I am to them. I guess it would be a good thing if we all felt lucky to be who we are.

How's that for inspiration?

Home

Los Angeles, June 1968

◆ ◆ ◆

The night RFK got gunned, we'd been lounging about our room at the Cambridge Arms on Sunset navigating a quart of Cutty Sark, playing cards, listening to the radio when the news broke. Damnedest thing, the gunning. To a man, we all had mountain spring, crystal clear memories of where we were when his older brother got clipped in Dallas. And here we were again, making new indelible memories of where we'd been when we first heard the incredible news.

"Helluva thing."

There were four of us in the room with two beds, and anyone could have said any one of these things. Every one of us was thinking it.

"Now the fuck what?"

"What the fuck now is right."

We tucked into a new bottle, eyeing the remaining ones, listening to the news unspool.

"Is he dead or what?"

"Doesn't sound like it, does it? They made a mess of him in the kitchen, and now he's probably in some white room with the docs."

"My money says he doesn't make it."

No one wagered.

The radio crackled hysterically.

"How old's old lady K? Must be in her 70s."

"She's lost a lot of her boys. In the service of God and Country."

"To God and Country!"

Hear-hears. Clinks. Quiet.

"So where does this leave us?"

"Where does this leave us is damned right."

"I'm keeping my scratch no matter what."

"We're not there yet. We'll wait this out and see what we can see. Then we'll make a phone call and go from there."

"I already got designs for what I've already got and getting."

"We'll make that call when the time's right."

"It's not looking like we're getting him in the City of Angeles. We're gonna have to get him in Chicago. At the earliest."

"Let's not worry about that now."

"I'm just saying someone's eating our fucking lunch and we're sitting here like a pack of fools drinking and listening to the radio like we're on vacation."

"Listen, that punk that popped him got nabbed and is now getting rubber-hosed downtown. You want to get up close and personal, you just march yourself down to that hospital and finish this thing off. As for the rest of us, we're doing this thing the way we were paid to do this thing. From a distance. At our discretion. And walking away from it. So, if you don't stop flapping your yapper, I'll do it for you. Gratis. I have no qualms about that. None whatsoever."

We drank some more. Ran low on cigarettes. Walked out into the Los Angeles night among the strange murmuring crowds that milled in groups as if killing time along a parade route.

We went to an all-night cafeteria. Different groupings. Same murmurings.

We got the cigarettes.

We got back to the room.

Took turns sleeping.

Took turns listening to hospital updates.

Like faithful night companions on a long night of solemn vigil.

By 9:00 a.m., we were reasonably rested.

We took turns showering.

The radio updates were monotonous. "He's not coming out of this."

We left the room with a five-dollar bill tucked under a lamp and the radio running.

We drove out of the city into the desert toward Vegas, gloomily.

The Bitter End

A Swift Kick to the Cubicles

◆ ◆ ◆

I was in the lunchroom eating a microwaved beef and cheese burrito. The center was molten hot, as you'd expect from a six-minute radiation shower. I wasn't paying attention when I was jabbing at the buttons. I was watching that twit Gerald and that mocha-brown cocktease Bernadette sitting at the table by the window, trying to act nonchalant while everyone knows what's what. She was a cocktease, no doubt about it. And a lotta cocks don't like to get teased, you know? 'specially after a hundred dollars or something of food and drink. She was that kind, for sure. So as the skin on the roof of my mouth felt like it was sloughing off, I was trying to act cool about it, but that little game of office foreplay wasn't cooling things down for me.

That's always the goddamned way with me.

I have my limitations. I get that. And I have the luck of a blade of grass in a dog park. I get that too. I don't want to be reminded of my limitations in life or luck, as if the cataloguing and indexing of my limitations were somehow a favor that helps me overcome those limitations. To a kid, we say it's cruel and outright abusive to constantly remind that kid that he's more than a lotta bit of a loser. The kid gets that. But that doesn't mean he wants to hear about it every day.

Kids grow up. They go off and do things. School. Independence. Then stuffed right into a work funnel. Hooray.

Got to go get that money.

I hate being someone's wage monkey. Wages at any level, monkeys of any size and hue and stink. I couldn't stand the thought of some feckless fuckball who's never had an original notion giving me "feedback" on my performance. I get I'm not the best employee imaginable. If I were, I'd be running this fucking place, wouldn't I? So spare me the concerned tones about my career trajectory, meaningless comparative numbers, and mentoring me up with that nutless Gerald. (I almost stabbed that little fucker with a pen once.)

Let me backtrack. I understate "couldn't stand." It was closer to a homicidal rage because sitting in that office with some ... little twerp ... a person I wouldn't piss or shit on if he was on fire or starving to death. He wore his authority ugly. So used to being flattered and deferred to and bathed in such TLC. It makes for unattractive character traits. Pompous, entitled, a jerk. And me, what could I do? What was I going to say? My opinions don't mean a goddamned thing. Like a fucking feudal lord, he is, his powdered, perfumed balls hanging over me in judgment. And he's enjoying it, I could tell. I probably would, too. But that doesn't make it right.

The long and skinny: I'm reduced daily to some tool to be maximized for optimal performance. I don't want to be optimized. I get it—you'll tell me (unhelpfully) *shit, son, you don't like getting paid to do stuff, don't do stuff. Go starve. Go start your own company. Shit, they're doing your talent-free ass a favor as it is.* Like I said, that isn't helpful in the slightest. It's going to make me madder than I already am. It's going to want me to get on the national evening news, if you catch my drift.

But he's not the only one. Only the face of the beast. I have a list. It's a long list of suck-ups and bullshitters and backstabbers and overachievers. And I don't give any more fucks. That performance-reviewing little prick's five-dollar words are still in my head. Optimization. Goal-oriented. Alignment. Team-focused. Fungibility. Furlough. Like little needles, they're in my head reminding me they're there. They were the final five straws. And believe me, that little optimization fucker was going to be the first to go because there was NO WAY that cunt was going to hide or run away once the party starts. I was going to shoot him in the mouth. Not one word of explanation. Just POP. I was going to make Dostoevsky's guy in *Notes from Underground* seem like a mildly angst-ridden human being in comparison.

Because what are my alternatives, really? What's left? It's not crying, I'll tell you that much. Laughter?

You know who makes me laugh? Tarantino. He looks and acts like a twitchy high-school loser who made good with his funny bone and imagination. He's channeled his rage into comic-book violence and gets to be cool. He was smart enough not to be someone's wage monkey for very long.

I tried the Tarantino approach for a spell. This morning. It didn't work. Nothing at all cartoonish about the violence there.

Now I'm leaning against a glittering white commode, breathing hard from a vanished thrill, shot (how many times?), bleeding to death, I guess. I didn't think the police would show up so quickly. They're fricking fast! Like you wouldn't believe fast. Well, they're outside the door now. I can hear them. If they came barging in, I'd let them finish me off. I got nothing against them.

A hell of an end. A real glorious end—resting against the porcelain wall of a hole in space into which people pinch and flush their shit into eternity, never to be seen or thought of again.

Perfect.

Just fucking perfect.

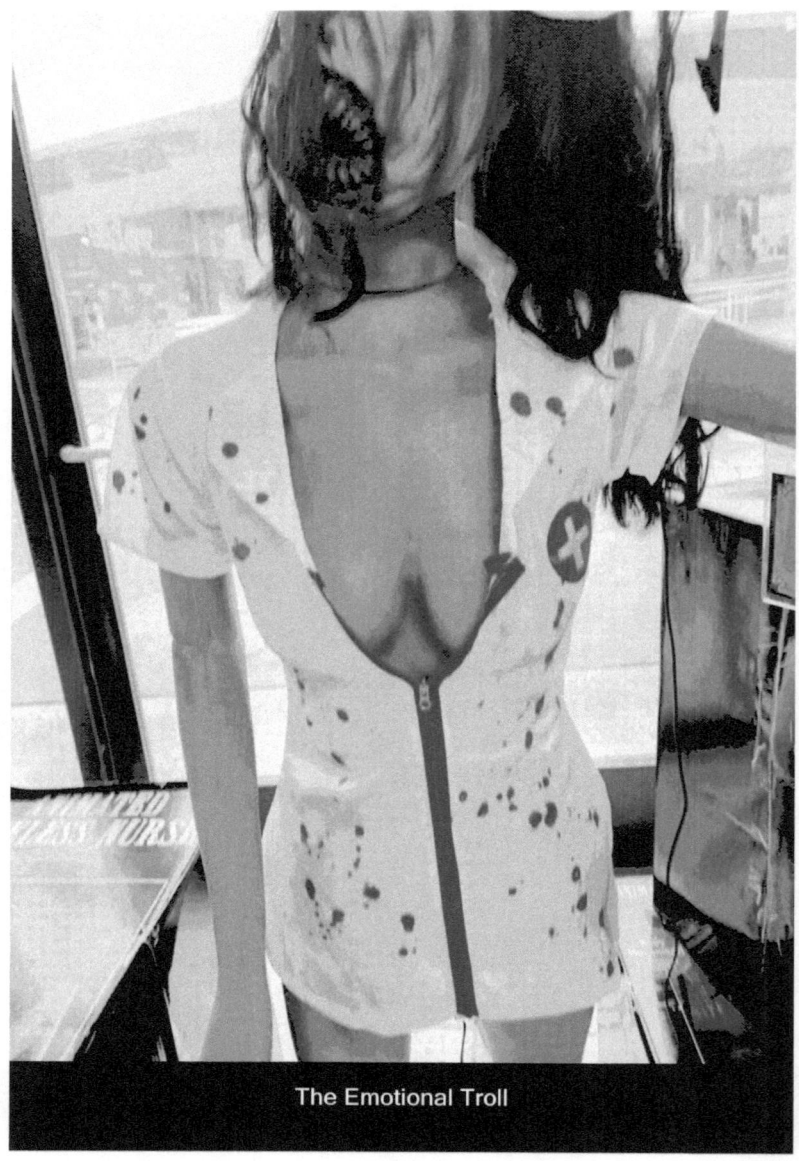

The Emotional Troll

Readbait: A Story About Hot, Sticky Porn

◆ ◆ ◆

"**T**his isn't a deposition, and I'm not on trial here, so I don't do questions. Just to politely reclarify. You guys ready?

The woman and man sitting across the coffee table from him nodded in unison.

"OK. Click it."

The woman clicked the recorder on.

"Every cup'la years you *Times* people come out our way to gauge the temperature of us smut people. Keeping up with the zeitgeist, I guess. And it sells papers, I guess. Right? Anyway, a cup'la years back, it was the HIV thing with the talent, if I remember right. And before that, there was the underage thing. And on and on. Listen, I don't give a shit of a whit. Any publicity is good publicity, right? Anyway, you can edit out what you want from what I'm going to say, but I'm in the scripted storytelling business, and I wouldn't have it any other way.

"That being said, here's my backstory. My father was crystal clear about one thing in his life. "Don't defend a woman's honor, you damp squib," he'd say to me, "defend her rights. Do that all that the time, and you'll get laid all the time." That was what we Californians like to call his mantra. But think about it. That was some pretty progressive shit he was saying if you think about it. And he was saying that shit in the '70s.

"He was a pussyhound from the old school—the buffed bod, the deep Miami Beach tan, the shag rug chest hair, the gold necklaces, the giant pinky rings, the wad of cash to choke a mine shaft. The smokes and highball. The mile-long Detroit car. He was the root from which the cliché sprouted to cinematic brilliance. Or maybe it was the other way around. He was prolly around before Burt Reynolds crashed the scene. I haven't done the math. The girls were on that horny hound of a father of mine like fleas. He treated them with such grace, respect, and equanimity they wouldn't stop hanging around even when he was banging some other young up and comer. You guys see *Boogie Nights*?

The two reporters nodded again.

"Man. Beautiful work. Too much, too much sweetness there. It's a perfect piece. That's pretty much how it works. Then and now. But now, with distribution the way it is, there's loads more money to be had. More competition, sure. But you make stuff people want to pay for, and guess what? They pay you money for the stuff they want.

"Everyone knows this. Not a problem. That's why there's an endless supply of young people willing and able to give us the goods. I give zero shits and even less fucks why they come out here to me. Me? I'm not a psychologist, or sociologist, or anyone's father confessor. You want to get fucked and jizz and get jizzed on camera for money, let's talk. These aren't damaged kids with mommy and daddy issues. Not any more or any less than kids applying for any other job. Anyone who tries to tell me that every kid who applies to one of these Santa Monica tech firms is a perfectly adjusted young adult can kiss my balls. There is a line out my door, across the valley floor, all the way out to LAX of fine young things all ready to take my money.

"It's just another way to make money. There is no porn crisis in this country, no crisis in licentiousness. We're not going the way of the Rome of Caligula. There's no Moral Majority because there is no sinner minority class. There are, what, seven billion people on this planet at this very moment, each one conceived in a mini, probably unfilmed, porn episode. What there is, is different groups of people trying to make a buck off the same thing, but from different sides—the sex industry and the hilarious anti-sex industry. The way I do it is a lot, lot simpler, with lots less lies and headaches. It's nice to get your sex without the sanctimony.

"You guys know who my father just despised more than anything in the world?"

The two reporters shook their heads.

"Phyllis Schlafly. I mean, here was a woman working her damnedest to make sure other women remained nothing more than glorified jizz receptacles. And unpaid, I should add.

What complete bullshit. My father gave loads of money to the Equal Rights Amendment people. Yeah, those hairy droopy-tittied feminists weren't his thing, but, like I said, you got to fight for a woman's rights. He got laid at those conventions like you wouldn't believe.

"I have great admiration for the young women who work for me. I give out scholarships to my girls. Did you know that? It's part of their incentives package. Know why? 'Cuz I want them to leave here and go off to college—if they want—and tell their hot young girlfriends that the money to be made here in my operations ain't such bad money. It's smart business, really. And it keeps me in the pink, so to speak.

"Now … Are there bad operators out here? Hell, sure, like in every industry imaginable. Young women have to make a choice. I try to steer them to the better choice whenever they ask for my two cents. Republicans and Democrats and churches and rights groups and all that horseshit can bitch and moan all they want about the immorality of the so-called 'adult entertainment industry,' but I'm not giving the time of day to anyone who thinks the likes of Bill Clinton, Newt Gingrich, Donald Trump, Pat Robertson, Gloria Steinem, or any ass-raping fuckstick in the Catholic Church hold a molecule of moral righteousness in their sticky little fingers. They are all filthy money- and power-collecting smegma. At least people like me have the balls to say we film young people fucking, and we sell that film of young people fucking to anyone who has money to buy it.

"Listen, life is exactly like a porn shoot: you show up, say a cup'la things no one remembers, bang hard, bang long, get paid, go home. Everything else is mental masturbation. That's life.

"OK. My sermon script's over. There is nothing I want to add or retract. Please feel free to quote me as you see fit. Done."

He stood up and stretched. The woman clicked the recorder off. The reporters stood.

He took two cellophane-wrapped Blu-ray discs off the table and thrust them into their hands. They reflexively took what was handed them.

One of the Steps of Your Journey

Young Love

◆ ◆ ◆

The doorbell rang. I waddled over to the window and looked down. Two spiffy-looking men were at the front door, standing stupidly in a steamy Carolina drizzle. No umbrella, no nothing. Parked along the curb, their rectangular box of a car screamed police. I'd seen enough TV to know the setup. The long raincoats probably made them homicide detectives.

Fucking Kevin. Let me stick the tip in, he'd said. A real romantic charmer. *What would be the harm*, I thought. Just the tip. I'm the stupid one. In ten seconds, he was thrusting, and shaking, and making male porno sounds. Twenty seconds after that, he wanted me to be quiet for a bit. Now look at me. There's no chance of me going to Clemson. Everyone else is getting ready for a crazy summer before college. Then who knows what they'll be up to once they get to college? Just Google "college party" and you can pretty much see the future. But I'll be sitting right up here with my new bundle of joy. I don't say "our" because old Kevvy started making himself super scarce after I told him I was knockers. Started not answering his phone. Started answering me with *yeah yeah* and *I guess*. Then he stopped coming around after my parents made me stay at home. They weren't even pissed at him. Didn't even call his parents, I don't think. They got me these big, billowy tent dresses for me to grow into and we pretend I'm an immaculate virgin who's never seen a dick tip up close. They've got about another two months before they'll need to adjust to a new reality.

A lot more than my virginity got pricked that afternoon. I felt something other than a baby filling up inside of me. Kevin's crazy if he thinks I'm forgiving him his sins. Just batshit crazy. He can ignore and pretend all he wants. I did the math. There was absolute zero point zero zero percent chance he was getting away from me. No way. I sent him a Snapchat with a nice oiled shot of my giant boobs and puffy nipples. *Wanna see these?* Send. *Hell yeah I wanna see those.* Reply. That's what I thought. *Meet me 2morrow. noon at our place and bring the blanket!* I just gotta hope he kept his pimply, horny trap shut. I'm a praying girl. So, I've got the faith.

The TV shows would say what I did to him in the corner room of Butterfield Mill was premeditated. Baa bum. Sort of. I was planning on stabbing him a lucky seven times, but went overboard with eleven. I waddled right up to him, rubber gloves on my hands, boobies bouncing, flouncing, him with that grin of yummy anticipation I'd seen before, and jabbed him all those times in his fleshy side. Kidney, liver, spleen, stomach—I don't know what got what, but something caused him to scream and swear, then fall over in a ball, which made it kinda easier for me. That's probably why I went to eleven from my knees. Then I took the blanket and phone away from him and left. Didn't even look back. Didn't hear anything. Didn't want to hear anything.

That was four, five days ago. You know what? I haven't felt any regret at all. Was he feeling regret for knocking me up, then taking off and having his fun like nothing at all happened? Or planning his future without giving me a moment of thought? No and no. So I wasn't going to feel guilty, either. Nope. Stabbing someone eleven times might seem like a crazy thing to do. And it kinda was. But you know, I'm not even scared. I now feel like I can do anything! I can even raise this baby on my own if I have to. And now Greenville's finest is at my door. So, my guess is they found him, because his parents started raising a stink on Sunday morning when they hadn't seen their precious darling since the day before. *Oh, I haven't seen or spoken to him in a few weeks. I hope he's okay. Tell him to call us when he gets back.* Yes, me and their grandbaby are terrifically worried about him.

So I'm looking down at the front door and these two characters are waiting for me to open the door for them. Let's see what they've got on me. A young woman in my condition needs time to get where she's going. We're going to put on a good show. We're going to have our own reality show—*Murderous Southern Baby Mamas*. Yes, we are. And when this baby boy is born, if I'm still a free girl, I'm going to name him Kevin. A delicate thing with postpartum whatever in deep mourning has got to keep up appearances.

Youth in Flight

Saint Tiller

◆ ◆ ◆

Tiller melted into the crowd, just another among so many others. But I stood watching after him, almost perplexed at how easily, how quickly, he slipped and bled away, even as my eyes remained focused, attentive. I didn't want to believe it—not really—and I stood on my tiptoes trying to re-catch a sighting, a glimpse of the top of his head. Maybe. Nothing. I lowered my heels to the ground. I looked around for something familiar. And it was all so. The fairgrounds. The game stalls. The sounds. The smells. My parents nearby laughing at something Mr. Jenkins might or might not have said. A strange sight, really. The laughter. But Mr. Jenkins was funny, either way. And puny Jonesy Fuller standing at a distance, staring at me. Blankly. Not as strange. He didn't like girls too much. And the blue July sky that framed and contained us all. I hoisted again onto the tip of my toes and looked out. This time slowly, patiently. But Tiller stayed gone.

By the time Tiller returned home, we had had our supper, I had bathed, dressed in cotton shorties, sitting on my heels on the chair at the table, playing cards with Dad in the kitchen. Mom stood at the sink, watching us. The screen door opened, and just as quickly snapped shut, the sharp sound like a rifle shot, then reverberation. Mom jumped, her eyes wild, searching for a moment. Then calmness. She wiped her hands on the apron. I looked up and over my shoulder, waiting for my brother to walk down the hallway and into the kitchen.

He did.

And everyone smiled.

Tiller stood in the doorway. A silence—a soothing silence—froze us in place for the briefest of moments, like a ceremonial moment of appreciation, impromptu, not forced, before Mom's voice refocused my attention away from the door.

"I can warm you up a little something if you're still hungry."

Tiller walked across the intricate linoleum mosaics toward Mom, as if he wanted to hand-deliver his answer to her question.

He leaned against the sink. "No thanks, Mom. I really am full. But tomorrow … breakfast, lunch, and dinner."

Mom reached her hand out, extending her index finger, and let it tap the tip of Tiller's nose. "Okay. All your favorites." That's how she was.

"All my favorites."

Dad dragged the chair from under the table, wiping the seat briskly. "Come on, here. Join us for a game or two." Tiller looked at the table and the piles of cards we'd formed. "War?" Dad nudged the edges of the downturned cards by his hand. "Mmm hmm. But we can play anything you'd like." Tiller looked at me and winked, the right side of his mouth curling up. "I'll referee the two of you. Keep everyone honest." Tiller eased into the chair, as Mom stepped behind him, resting her hands in one another, tightly against her chest. They watched as Dad and I played card after card onto the discard pile, with me trying to avoid war, and Dad playing through the war-inducing matched cards. I didn't mind. I wasn't thinking of winning or losing. I think we wanted to sit there in our own small silence.

I was in my bed, turned on my side, watching the open and empty case at the end of Tiller's empty bed, waiting for him to come in. Outside, there were sounds in the distance, fading and transitory, as if moving on their own in the dark; fireworks maybe, car horns blowing, the sounds joyous people make. Inside the house, I stared unblinkingly at the closed bedroom door, until I heard the door to Mom and Dad's room open, some whispered, indistinct words, then the door closing. Footsteps, in no particular rush, along the floorboards. My eyes relaxed, closed for a moment, then opened as the door opened.

Tiller in his nightshirt walked in. "Hey! Am I keeping you up?" He was whispering, slowly closing the door behind him.

"No. Just waiting on you."

He walked around to the bureau and opened the top drawer. He removed one pair of knotted socks. And stopped, looking at the remainder, as if he didn't have the heart to remove any more. I watched him from the pillow. He removed a leather-bound journal, placing it next to the sock.

"Are you scared?"

He put the sock back in the drawer. Then the journal. He closed the drawer. "No, not anymore."

"How come?"

Tiller moved to the end of the bed, pushing the case away, sitting down. "Because I've stopped trying to imagine bad things."

"Like what?"

Like what.

Tiller remained quiet for a moment—sad—as if my question had made him imagine again what he didn't want to imagine. Which was true, I think, because he said, "I've sort of trained myself, you know, practicing to put it out of my head. Think of this room, maybe. Or Mom and Dad ... the guys and the ball field ... our bicycles. You know ... just anything so not to ... " Tiller was looking at me.

"I know ..."

"I knew you'd know. You're too smart."

I smiled at him, not really believing him, but wishing it were true. I didn't know. And I didn't know what I didn't know.

"So, you're not scared."

"No."

I paused, wondering if I should say what I really wanted to say. I think it might have been the brave thing to do, not to say what I wanted to say. But I don't think I wanted to hide from my brother. Not at that moment.

"But I'm scared, Till."

He stood and moved over to my bed, sitting at my side. And without a word, he adjusted the pillow, then eased his head into its softness, stretching his long, thin frame along the edge of the small bed. "Come on."

I, too, eased my head back onto the vacant corner of the crowded pillow. I stared off at the ceiling, the two of us probably looking at the same spot. I closed my eyes. For a moment.

"I promise to be here."

"Me, too," he said.

How much time had passed? The electric ceiling light hummed, the darkness past the window remained a calm, inky pool. The curtain, a barely perceptible sway. Quiet. Hush. Peace. Tiller stirred, his hand moving quickly, violently, precisely against an imagined pest resting on his cheek. He swept the phantom away, his calm undisturbed. His arm retreated, resting across his stomach. It rose and fell slowly. I watched, my mind recalling Sunday school lessons resting inertly behind a dense fog borne of boredom and inattention of wasted Sunday mornings. I reached and reached, thought and thought.

Saint Christopher. Maybe.

But I didn't know. I couldn't remember.

"Dear God, now I lay me down …" No. I didn't know. I couldn't remember. Tiller stirred again, made sleep sounds. I froze. Waiting. Melting. Then whispered, "Good night, Till." I turned my head again and watched the ceiling. I wanted to see something crawling up there, something to keep me company, something to count, but I couldn't imagine that, either.

It was a nice day. Sun and warmth and the train's idling breath. Tiller's smiling face was among the five or six or seven soldiers jostling for one final glimpse from the train window onto the platform. Where Mom, Dad, and I stood in a row, waving. Other parents and children waved. And waved. And the train jolted, hesitated, and our heads turned in anticipation. And my mother buried her face in my father's shoulder. And the train moved, and Tiller's face moved with it, smiling still, and my Sunday school memories came back from the night before, St. Christopher wanting to speak, if that was him, and I not having any words to place in his mouth, there in my head. The train found its rhythm, moving faster now, Tiller gone down the track with it, and Dad pulled me around the shoulders into his stomach. And it felt so, so good.

The news came in dribs and drabs. Radio, newspapers, rumors. Dad had his map. Mom had her silent and patient worry. Then a letter! A letter!! "And tell Daisy I miss her. Tell her I think about her all the time. I've got all sorts of fun stuff for her." Where was he? Dad showed me on the map. "He was here and now I think he's over here somewhere." It was a long way from where he'd been. And the only place I'd been since was to school and back. But it added up.

As did the days and weeks and months. All the same, really, except I knew more. The war was all about us, like a years-long fair no one attended. In school. At home. At play. Falling asleep. And in Jonesy Fuller's older brother coming home for burial. He died fighting Germans with the English for the Dutch in Holland, also called The Netherlands. We

learned that in school. And I had come to know of the serious-
ness of the world at hand. Jonesy now stood even further away
from all the others. He may even have liked girls by then. I
didn't know. I didn't ask. Or maybe I didn't want to know.
And in church, more than once a week, I found the missing
voice in my head. A prayer to keep our Tiller safe. A prayer
for the war to end. All in my voice. And a St. Christopher
pendant in my pocket, identical to one we had sent Tiller in a
package with gums and socks and letters and a few books he
could carry around in his pockets.

More boys … died there as 1944 gave way to 1945. They
returned here in wood boxes. I sat in the same class room with
some of their sisters. I didn't want to be in there. With them.
Or anyplace else. I didn't want to live in that town anymore,
imagining life near an ocean with boats to sail out on, but
Dad told me there would be no place to go. No place could be
any different. They'd all be the same. And Mom agreed, still
silent, still with the patient, patient, patient waiting in her
eyes. "We'll be here for when Tiller gets back." That seemed
less fair than it did right, because I couldn't imagine fairness.
There was only rightness. I could see beyond the moving pictures of the picture shows, the ones that showed people of all
ages and shapes in donkey and horse carts going places. They
never showed up where we were, so they must have still been
out there on the move. But I knew what drove them away. I
did. I knew it was the same thing that sent those poor dead
boys back home to their parents. Dead for a long time. I didn't
feel like playing, really. I read, though. I read about all the

places Dad told me Tiller must have been. France in 1914 had had another war. So had Belgium. And Germany, too. The library had these books. I scribbled numbers on a piece of paper. It didn't seem like 32 years was such a long time. Memories must have been short.

Our memories were about to be shortened, too. Victory in Europe led to a similar one in Japan. And a parade. And free ice cream sundaes at the pharmacy. And firecrackers almost every day, as boys returned and returned. And one day, just like that, the front screen door opened and snapped shut, still like the rifle's shot. Mom's "Jesus Mary" was barely audible over Tiller's "Mom. Dad. Daisy." I don't know nor remember how I got to the front door. I don't. But I did. And had to wait in the short line to grab at Tiller, my brother. I hugged him for a very long time.

It could have been two nights later, maybe more. I lay in bed waiting for Tiller. Mom had turned down the covers of his bed and had placed a few salty crackers there "to settle his stomach." He finally walked in, closing the door behind him. He was already in his pajamas. He came around to the end of my bed and sat down. I sat up.

"Were you scared, Daisy?"

"I don't know."

He placed his hands in his lap, rubbing them together. "I thought of you every day."

"Me too!"

"Whenever I had a chance, I said a prayer for you, Daisy. And Mom and Dad, too." He paused, and I thought he smiled at something. I looked out after his dim smile, then back at him. "To get you through, to get you across."

"We're here."

"We are. We got across. We're back."

Tiller stood, then bent to kiss my forehead. "Good night, Daisy."

"Good night, Till."

He moved across the way, gently placed the crackers on the table between the beds, got under the covers, and was asleep before I could find anything more to say. I watched him sleep. Then I slid the crackers off the table, one at a time, and chewed as quietly as I could.

Time is nothing to itself, playing itself out all the while starting anew. But I have to remember from the beginning for the both of us now because Tiller can no longer remember for himself. Not anymore. My memories start when he left and when he came back. I remember the prayer I had in my mind, the one in my voice, the one I first wrote with ink on paper to memorize, repeated daily, then came to believe—to know— would come true. And it did come true. And I am very grateful. I can still breathe my prayer just as easily as I did then.

"God? Please take me along with my brother. Take me to when he needs me most of all. Take me along to the places he never thought he would go. Please take me to where we can be together. I may not be much help, I may not know what to say, I may not want to be there, but please let me go. Please let him know I'm there, even though I will wait for him over here as well. Just as I promised.

"If that is too much to ask, then please end this war. Please make my mother and father and everyone else you can imagine happy by ending the war. Nobody would miss it. Nobody would wish it to come back. There's no sense in keeping people apart. There would only be happy people who'd thank you in their prayers and in their songs at church. I would be there, too. I've been paying a lot more attention in Sunday school, too. I think this would make me the happiest person there is. Amen."

But mostly, I remember that Tiller went and came back. And maybe we all went, and we all came back. I liked being back, Tiller there in the room with me even after we, one by one, grew older and moved to houses down the street from one another. Mom and Dad went, just as we're going. But there is still more time, still more time for memory and places to go. There is no missing in time, not time done fairly, time as it ought to be, the going away and coming back until that last and final time. I think it was in the coming back that we do the best by one another. We allow time to do its thing, and we do our best to do ours together.

I fed him his favorite minestrone soup tonight and watched him sleep. He had asked me again what this thing in his sweater pocket was for. I moved to his chair and took the St. Christopher pendant in my hand. "This is what you are to me."

He nodded. I placed the pendant back in his pocket. "You keep that there, okay?"

And like he always does, he smiled faintly, kindly at something that really wasn't there, smiling at something from his long, long ago. I will try to remember this as well.

Holding on to Potential

Cruelty

◆ ◆ ◆

It's tricky, but in the end, when it comes, the only thing that'll have mattered will probably be love—the giving and receiving of it. It's important to keep the giving and receiving of love at as stable an equilibrium as possible to avoid an encounter with someone like me. I'm not a bad man, not in the strictest definition of the word, not in my mind, not in the mind of those who are left to me, not by the actions that precede me. I'm a bad man because I know what I do is not the right thing. The wrong thing. There are no redeeming virtues to my labors. I judge other people's actions, document their lack of fealty, destroy whatever shred of civility that may exist between two people, collect my money, go home. I have no unnatural attachment to money; it's a comfortable subsistence-plus arrangement. My expenses are meticulously documented, my time valued with a reasonable markup, with no room for an inflated sense of importance. My clients tell me they appreciate that. And I tell them I appreciate prompt payments. They have the luxury of being late with my money exactly one time. I tell them that, too. There are no problems here. The problems are out there.

This is my introduction, my calling card, as they pass through my door into the shadows they think I live in. Sit down, please. You may call me Lance, or Mr. Boyle, or nothing at all. Your choice. Then an attentive silence from me. The unraveling of a life unfolds before me—duplicity, depravity, avarice, retribution, punishment, humiliation ... weakness. There is very, very little variation. I've taken my notes, gauged the complexity and time commitment, quoted a minimum fee. There can be no further action on my part prior to a twenty percent retainer fee hitting my till. I can wait no longer than Wednesday. My apologies. I answer questions patiently, and they have many, then ease them out of the office and into a damp San Francisco morning to be alone with their reflections. We are then each alone with our reflections. I swivel into my solitude, the chair creaking under my reclined weight, gazing out the window through a fast-moving mist onto the bay and its gray bridge, living the cliché happily, wondering about other men in other times, real and fictional. There is no mystery, nor romance, nor glory to the grayscale world of operatives, maybe the second oldest profession, maybe developed to keep the ledgers on the oldest. I try not to waste time abstracting my reality unduly, although I'd like to believe I have all the time in the world.

Most prospects return on their own impatient volitions, re-darken the doorway with less hesitancy, ease themselves back into the chair opposite me, place the cash retainer reverently on the desk, wait for a physical accounting which doesn't come, ready themselves to further elaborate on their injustices upon request. It's a one-sided prompted conversation of love worn and done. I have nothing to add or subtract. I take what's given. It's what I work with. Movements, habits, tastes, weaknesses, addresses, suspicions, missing money, misplaced trust, the list could continue—the human condition is embedded in the strains of our relationships, what had once been hoped for, what it had become. Decisions made and regretted, abandoned and resuscitated, only to be abandoned again, never reaching me in their flowering. It's the only way I've come to imagine it. For the most part, we seem incapable of divining poor character from good for reasons that perpetually defy. Maybe hopeful-ness, maybe ignorance, maybe naïveté. Have I been jilted of fees and good graces? Most certainly. Lied to, manipulated, duped? Without a doubt. There is no lasting shame attached, a lesson learned, repeated later in a different incarnation. A piece of the whole. The connection between any two people may just as eas-ily be wedded to fallacy and avarice as to truth and honor. It is as natural as the connection itself. There is no point in justify-ing yourself and your actions to me, just as there is no sanity in vilifying the other. I have already taken sides, and here is your receipt. It is a part of the original parcel, you getting to me before the other. What you want from me, I say, is the anecdotal of what you allege. Correct?

Yes.

Thank you for your time. I'll be in touch with regular updates and invoices.

We move in the open, most of us observed, but not remembered. I am paid to watch and remember. To be found and recorded is simplicity personified. There are no secret places; there have never been any secret places. Even your thoughts are betrayed by your actions. You are nowhere at any time, just as surely as you are somewhere at all times. This is neither abstraction, nor empty words. This is what a man like me does, at the behest of someone who may have once loved you.

I look out the window. Blankly.

A container ship seemingly inches along the surface of the bay, away from Oakland and its monstrous cranes, angling north by northwest, taking all the time it needs to pass through the Golden Gate, when the telephone rings. I answer. And listen. It's one of my operatives in the field, down the coast past Pacifica, calling to check in. He's taken a lead into a dead end. People lie, it's to be expected, I say, but with considerably less couth. Come on home.

"She should be here. She told him she'd be here," he continues, pleadingly. He's young, been on the job for a year and some, still assigned the follow-and-sniff stuff. He lost her. There'll be another day. He'd find her again.

What more could I say to him? We learn not by being told, not really. Besides, he'll get paid regardless.

"We'll get her tomorrow. Come on home." Tomorrow's always another glorious day.

I hang up the phone and look out the window again, lost leads and dead ends easy thoughts to have. We've gotten too familiar with it all, comfortable with what's come to be

expected, an unassailable sign of professional proficiency—
the pilot reacting to a wicked shimmy while climbing his craft
in a thunderstorm, the center fielder nonplussed by the tight
inside fastball, the cop facing down his fourth flailing drunk
of the night. But to what end? We race to where? And at what
price?

The kid down there in Pacifica has the easiest of jobs, an
obvious and almost gratuitous infidelity, the kind the young
ones always sharpen their teeth on. The husband had come in,
distraught in moderation to his anger, a vengeance unmod-
ified from any that may be found in ancient scriptures; an
unforgiving sort, I could tell. A straight-line narrative. The kid
down there will come to learn what we've all come to learn,
with little discernable variation. In his due time.

The container ship is passing from view, starting its Pacific
journey on rough seas. Fare thee well.

People lie. It's to be expected. The world of lies is a prag-
matic one, and a lazy one, of limited face value, theatrical in
its machinations, all the world its stage, the bit parts barely
noticed. It's easy enough, a symptom of a putrid gangrenous
disease, rotting—literally rotting—the character to points of
raw bone and hardness, a Petri dish to test the postulation
that one's character is one's destiny. It's a game of consumption, every deception devouring, the belly swelling from the
gluttony of the feast. For what? For delusional gratification, an
addiction no different from the stiff drink or the cigarette or
anything else foisted on the endocrine system.

Or for a taste of the narcotic that is bad decisions.

The bay is empty and seemingly placid. But it's not, I know. The phone rings. I answer.

"Lance, it's set. We're good on Helms. In, out, easy." The voice is Hiram's, my friend and most experienced hand. We go back. He's a religious man, righteous of other men, devoid of personal scruples. Piously indifferent. A good Jesuit. Men like him are useful in the world.

"Swing by at seven. It's shaping to be a short night."

"Yeah, but we'll have some good streaming to keep us."

"Amen."

The line goes silent. I hold the phone for a moment, a dramatic pause for no effect. Then bring the receiver down. Arrogance is blinding. Weak, foolish, arrogant people convinced of their opaqueness and superiority. In this case, a Mr. John Helms has piqued the interest of his wife of years with his peculiar behavior. Dull to the point of sadness. It's taken us four days to break it. He thought it best to hide his dealings in the open. We record tonight at the near-empty rental they've been remodeling. Mrs. Helms will not be pleased. We meet with her tomorrow. Her sister will be in the footage. Silly, foolish, hurtful people.

It's impossible to walk the proverbial mile in someone else's proverbial shoes. Feigned empathy is the best we've got. I can imagine tonight's images. They're clear enough in the imagination. Hiram and I will watch remotely, ensuring the quality, angling in on faces, body parts, the graphics playing equally well in the sticky seats of smut theaters and the county courthouse. Mrs. Helms paid for thirty minutes of infidelity footage. I'll give her an hour's worth. She'll need it for emphasis. And tomorrow's conversation is already scripted, like an old favorite movie that's more familiar than good. We know what's to be done—the wicked shimmy, the high inside fastball, the drunk in our faces.

There's an ignorance that pervades, shockingly obtuse in its pervasiveness, a sense that if the thing is not thought through in its entirety it gradually ceases to exist. Avoidable consequences. So smart we are in the detailed work, the task-oriented drudgery in moment-to-moment specifics that pays for wanted things and rationalizes unconstructive debt in an instant. Continuously. And it's the same playlist with relations, the task-oriented work that leads to the hypocrisy of cruelty and betrayal, none of us amused or immune. It's a cheapness of spirit, ironic, really, in a reality awash in the mass of abundance. But this is what we've learned, what we've taught ourselves. A culture of so much built on the foundations of the utilitarianism of so little.

But this petulant, self-aware bitterness leads to nothing. I'm just marking my time with observations until it's my time.

So be it.

The phone rings again. I answer. It's Pacifica again.

"She's dead."

There's a long silence along the visible and invisible wires.

"Dead how?"

"Dead as in shot in the head. Twice. Maybe. Small caliber."

"Where are you?"

"I came 'round to the backyard. She's back there, against the shed."

My lips feel chapped, my mouth dry. My fingers move to the base of my nose, thinking.

"Retrace your steps out of there."

"I'm outta there already. I'm on the sidewalk."

"Good boy. I'll call Hutchinson, he'll get Pacifica in there. Wait for them in the car."

I hang up the phone.

"Goddamn it!" These are my words into an empty room.

My client will prove to be a killer of the most ordinary variety, grossly unsympathetic, with no hope of extricating himself from himself despite delusions and anxieties. Where is he to go? And how long does he think it will take to get there? If this thing had gone down the way it could've gone down, two people would have found themselves divorced. And alive. The living have a way of surviving, obstinate in their relish for survival. Passionate. The dead don't. The dead don't, and there must be blame attached. And I will become part of the attachment.

I don't wait. I pick-up the phone and dial Hutchinson. He's the law. And the law is spoken to with different types of words. I articulate those words carefully, thoughtfully, and hang up the phone. I'll be seeing him often in the coming months. It's in the nature of these things.

I turn the chair back out toward the bay. It seems more comfortable, somehow. More mindful. I can't know Marlowe, of Chandler's disposition, as hard as this city—or as any city may be—I don't have the perspective of the post-trench, newly nihilist interwar life. It transcends the hardboiled callousness where deserving death came snappily and conveniently. There's no convenience to this thing, a world grown weary of causal and ideological death. I can make no truck with this thing, this suddenness of violence, this option forever on the corner of the table, so easily reached for, so mundane as to make it invisible, despite its potency and permanence.

Who are these people who keep themselves tethered to the past? What are we to make of them? How is any of this different than bringing forth in our collective name men of charlatan faith to wage savage wars of buffoonery, to allow black cities to drown, to reduce the infinitely complex to the child's parable of monsters under the bed, to lull us to sleep with full stomachs of disinterest? What are we to expect? The culture that rears us, buries us. And our markers are betrayal, callous cruelty, murder, and a warped sense of excusable righteousness. A fucked sense of certainty. We are wrong. I am wrong. How far will I go to absolve myself of blame? Am I the wicked man who has wrought wrong? Am I the man who has shed daylight on an undershadow of wickedness? Am I the bullshit righteous man I belittle?

"Jesus!" My spoken word is startling, shocking. Weirdly, I wait, but the room remains quiet. I can't think of another word to say. The day slips away, and I watch it.

There is composure again. And work to be done. I do it, like I'll always do it. It flows easily, like the river that erodes its banks into canyon. After a certain depth, it doesn't matter much. It becomes the natural order of things.

The early night comes, and Hiram drives slowly through the city. Neither of us speaks because there's nothing to say. Left, right, straight, right, left and we're there, someplace, like any other in a maze of a city, merely a Thursday night. We park. We wait. The monitor in my lap is small, the controls delicate and acutely responsive. In time, Mr. Helms enters the frame, tipping playfully onto the bed, removing his shoes. A woman's voice coos off-screen, teasingly as if by rote exercise, and Hiram looks out his window uninterested, maybe off someplace pleasant for the duration. But we are here, in this thing together, and there is no turning back for us. I tell myself it's just what we do. I watch intermittently, maintaining proper angles, focus, and professional integrity. And we do what it is we do for sixty minutes. As planned. Five would have sufficed, thirty paid for, but we get sixty. It's digitized and stored now for posterity and legal proceedings. I pack the machine back into its case.

"Done?"

"Yeah, done."

Hiram starts the car and pulls out into the near-empty street. People with no place to go must be staying home tonight. Hiram and I drive the city in silence.

It is quarter past ten when I walk through the front door. I ease it shut and draw the lock. The living room is dark. Eva is on the poorly lit balcony, a bottle of scotch, two empty glasses, and a sweating silver bucket of ice on the glass-top table. I walk out to her. I sit.

"How was it?"

I nod. "It was."

Eva leans across the table for a kiss. I meet her. We kiss for a nice while, her mouth tasting of the things the day lacked. She pulls back, pours the scotch into my glass, dropping two ice cubes in, lifting and tipping the ice bucket until the glass is full. She pours hers straight. Our glasses touch. We drink, looking at each other familiarly.

"They asleep?"

She smiles. "Probably not."

We drink once more, swallowing slowly. I stand and replace the glass. Eva does the same with hers. "Be back."

"Okay," she says and looks off into the night. I walk back into the dark living room, then down a dimly lit hallway to where our children should be sleeping, but are almost certainly not.

Beacon Beckoning

The Sh*t-end of the Stick

♦ ♦ ♦

The school day had ended with rocks being thrown at him, a routine of sorts that occurred nearly every day for no defensible reason, just one of those things. He stood steady there in the wood that led to his house. He'd tried running, hiding, throwing the thrown rocks back, but still they came, the rocks and childish invectives. This day would involve the improvised stick defense, the one where he'd take the biggest, most scarily knotted stick he could find and run at them. They'd run away as they had before; he'd go home. They'd meet again tomorrow or the day after.

It was still drizzling rocks, the muffled laughter and snorting insidious in its effects, as he readied himself for his defense, his gaze outward, bending at the knees for a three-foot-long stick, thick and sturdy, heavy among the autumn leaves and unruly blades of grass. Rising. But something wasn't right. The stick didn't feel barky, it felt more … chewy, viscous, alive. That's what he thought. He looked down at his clenched hand as it rose up, wincing, the stench reaching his nostrils, his physical body and immortal soul recoiling, all in near-simultaneous, unitary motion. He wanted to say *goddamn it*, wanted to bellow it, the way he'd heard his father say it, violently, but he didn't know what it meant. Not really. He dropped the foul-smelling stick and repulsively, instinctively wiped his hand along the length of his trousers, desperately, repeatedly. A rock hit him in the chest. A hooting erupted in the distance, a chorus of joyous disbelief. He looked out again, then down at the discarded stick, rubbing the impact point with his clean hand. It hurt. No more rocks came his way. He turned and walked away.

When he got home, trailing the stink smeared along the wrinkled seam of those trousers, he got—as his mother would later recount to his father—"his ass beat raw" as prelude, then, as dénouement, his nose shoved and held into the trousers his father had fished out of the hamper.

"That'll learn ya, goddamn it."

And there it was again.

He was in the bathroom for a long thirty minutes rubbing the tip of his nose and bathing the inside of his nostrils. It remained unscrubbed in his memory. Later, he lay in bed consciously breathing through his mouth, his eyes attached to a single spot on the ceiling. By the time sleep came, or just before, he was breathing through his nose again. He knew by morning, it wouldn't matter anymore anyway.

The first heavy rains came through that night, forming and readying themselves along the plains to the east, first coming in torrents of water, then later being cajoled by the altitude into snow. But on this night, he slept through the rains.

The snows of these high foothills have a wet quality, sticking to bare branches like a doughy paste sweeping away appendages past their prime, the ground trading its pastels for a soothing monochrome, vainly trying to tuck their restless wards into a winter-long slumber. Word would go forth from before dawn that roads had become impassable, schools had been canceled, telephone wires downed, an accident on Rural Route 12, a cat still unaccounted for. Snowfall and accumulation brought with it a brutal division of labor, the young to play, the able to toil, the hardened to carry on, the old to fret. In a long life's memory, all would be interchangeable. One had to be patient.

The first such snowfall came in the early morning hours in late November. He was awakened to all of this by his mother: "No school. Your father wants you dressed and outside." He felt hungry as he opened the door to face the out of doors. An uneven sea of white stretched across the field and into the trees. The mountains beyond looked shorter, yet more imposing, jutting as they did into the seemingly stagnant storm cloud cover. Black birds still flew. Two boys tugged at two toboggans, the rope over their shoulder, trudging in high snow toward a hill not so distant. His father's voice broke the dreamy hypnotic spell. "Get those shovels from the shack and clear the walk. Then start on the drive." He did as he was told, the shovel pressed against his stomach, pushing, a reasonably cleared path in his wake. The warmth built up beneath his layers, and the pain came as the shovel hit an uneven portion of the driveway driving the handle into his gut. *Goddamn it,* he thought, adjusting to the unevenness, pushing forth again. The handle would drive into his belly another half-dozen times before his labors were through. And later—much later—he would poke at the perfectly circled bruise just above his navel. But before that, still out in the elements, his father called out from the idling car, "I can get out now. I want to this drive looking like spring when I get back." His father drove forward slowly. He watched the exhaust climb, linger, then dissipate along the deformed piles of snow.

The sky darkened early. The corned beef stew tasted good. He slurped quietly from a spoon, watching the caged pepper grains through a clear glass shaker. His mother, in the other room, talked on the telephone. "I been trying to get a hold of him since six hours ago. He's yours during the day, so you tell me where's he at. It's ridiculous you can't tell me something as simple as that."

They found his father the next afternoon. He'd wrecked the car in a shallow ravine and probably survived, but then froze to death at night. The sheriff had seen such things before in that very place.

They buried him as best they could in the hard earth. His mother took the money from his sock drawer. It paid for the flowers.

Some indemnity came in, but not nearly enough to entice his mother away from the gas station. She continued on.

He left school for work at the meat cutting plant, a red-bricked relic from a gone age still relevant to those who needed it. Arcane laws from another time had long since attached themselves to the place, in their original form, more or less impervious to evolutionary impulses, made the place reasonably clean, reasonably safe, reasonably promising place for a boy of sixteen to be. It was good enough. Brooms, mops, and brushes are easily manipulated. And he worked hard, on his hands and knees, scrubbing the tiled floor like an anachronism, in the cold, cavernous interior, an immigrant charwoman as native man in some distant fin-de-some-siècle scenario. If such a thing were possible. Dickens revisited. He returned home smelling of piney disinfectant and entrails. He bathed slowly, meticulously, every square inch of skin attended to. He ate lightly and slept easily. The dawn took him back out again, six out of the seven days.

The worker who doesn't grouse rarely goes unnoticed, not the one using his fingernails to remove calcified blood from the grout between tiles, at least. "How'd you like to move on up to meat cutter? We can show you how, not a problem. Pays more, too. Then on to wrapping. And packaging. It's unlimited out there." They showed him how to cut, where to cut and how often, a few easy lessons, nothing to it, and placed him along an assembly line of other like-minded workers, quiet in the rote contemplation of their noisy labors, mechanical knives cutting through flesh and bone with industrial ease. Rest breaks disrupted the tedium of work, but his rhythm prevailed in his thoughts over the break, a body in motion tending to remain as such. At times, he'd stand in place over the work to be done throughout his 15-minute break. It didn't matter to him. He wasn't tired. He saw the angles of the grains, knew the force required for harmonious and efficient movement, depending on the cut, anticipating the woman standing to his left, aware of the pace of the other woman standing to his right, his force calibrated just so.

But he wasn't a machine. And the flesh slippery in its raw state. A misapplication of force in his focused state sent his right hand into the path of the vibrating teeth. At first there was a viscous, translucent silence and disbelief, suspended for a strange eternity, his words struggling to emerge through a miasma of stinging silence in his head—*oh, goddamn, goddamn, goddamn it* ... Nothing to it.

He staggered back from his position in the line, his left cupping his right, stanching the flow of blood from the three shorn knuckles, his pinky finger and thumb jutting out like saplings after a wildfire, turning to walk away, only to collapse on the floor a few steps away, his left hand giving way, his right slapping incomplete against the floor, his dulled eyes watching as his blood pulsed as if from three parallel drain pipes just beneath the knuckles, flowing along the subtly inclined floor toward the drain beneath the steel table, mingling with bovine blood, becoming indistinguishable, disappearing. Then welcomed darkness.

"There was never any realistic hope for reattachment. Not really. I'm sorry. Just too much nerve and tissue damage." This was the doctor to his mother. He was awake now, after three days of being out, but fatigued, fatigued. His mother sat in a chair opposite the bed, smiling intermittently, inquiring as to his pain levels. He felt a palpable heartbeat in a void.

"You'll have to learn to use the left one like you did the right one," she said once. And gave him a soft rubber ball.

He squeezed the soft rubber ball gently with his left hand, his mind nowhere in particular. The bed was comfortable, the nurses considerate. His mother would step outside the building to smoke a cigarette and something about seeing to a few things. He wouldn't see her for the rest of the afternoon. She'd return in the morning before work, then in the afternoon after it. They each had their lives to lead.

For the better part of a month, he was prayed for, whispered about with deep, tsk-tsking sympathy, the profile on the evening news showing a young man in his prime, cut down by outmoded machinery and a callous indifference to established norms of industry safety. Mountain Credit Union established a savings account for him, essentially a large container to drop change into; a human-interest story in the morning daily, an interview with a sympathetic labor relations official, legal minds of different motivations and skills paid courtesy calls, leaving behind brochures and promises of brave new worlds. The lingering could only last for so long. Collective memory ached to move forward. Populations still needed their meat cut, cleaned, packaged.

The better part of the month gave way to the cold winter of the month, where the shoots of memory fade, wither, die. He had left the hospital. The meat cutting proprietors settled with him for an undisclosed amount. He bought a reclining chair and a television, and reclined and watched television. Mountain Credit Union collected $114.25 and sent him a cashier's check. He, in turn, sent a thank-you note inside a colorful cardboard card written in a near-indecipherable scrawl. The thrift store mounted it behind a glass frame in their lobby.

A boy can lull himself to many points of pointless distraction, his days becoming identical. A girl can bring him back, refocus his purpose. A spring Tuesday proved a different day. She watched him before he saw her. She liked his calmness, sitting patiently in the waiting chair, holding a traumatized hand with the care of a new father, his face placid, an absent stare out of the heavy lids of blue eyes at nothing in particular, as if he were in some other place where, say, pain and worry and regret were quaint notions to be dramatized for effect, the slow, deliberate breathing, his chest rising and falling rhythmically.

She limped over to where he sat.

"Hello. I've heard about you. And read about you, too."

With that, she sat down. The talking came easy, an attachment to detachments that had been slowly evolving to define them each. She limped because her mother's dog's incisors and jaws had severed gastrocnemius nerves, if she was pronouncing that correctly. She didn't know much more than that, but he could sympathize, he told her, very much so, showing her his still-bandaged hand. She touched it gently, holding her fingertips to where his would have been, waiting, almost expecting to make it all better. That day—their first day—they waited for one another in the waiting room, then spent the afternoon in the backyard of his house, searching out similarities, glossing over differences, drinking beer from tall, sweating cans. The sun gloried through the wordy afternoon, an air of fate drifting through, peculiar in its light scent, convinced of its inevitability, the time before the dusk glinting across the cans playfully arranged in the tall grass, leaning haphazardly against blades a fraction their weight.

The talking moved to inside the house, and the talking merged into silence, a hot, desperate silence that found them on the floor, under a blanket and asleep as midnight came and went. In the morning, not far removed from the light's first break, she awoke, dressed and limped out of the house. An inglorious start to the day, but there were no alternatives. Jobs for her were hard to come by. Later, she wished she had left him a note. She knew what she would've said.

The September day she knocked on his door and called through the screen door, he instinctively thought her there to spend another afternoon together, a pleasant surprise that never failed to surprise. There could be no retracting the smile elicited by her voice calling to him. He opened the screen door, inviting her in, but she didn't move as she told him of her pregnancy. Probably by another boy. She couldn't be totally sure, but was pretty sure, and that she didn't know of any shameless way to tell him. She was sorry. Then she turned and ran unevenly to her car, idling roughly in the driveway. He stood watching out after her, long after she was no longer there. He wasn't thinking sad thoughts as much as he was thinking about her. He had hoped it would end differently, somehow, end with them together, the way they'd seen it, old and together, with many more afternoons in the backyard emptying tall beer cans. Instead, she'd be having someone else's child.

His mother moved two towns over with Frank, some older man, but left most of her belongings in the house. She returned at haphazard intervals for odds and ends, a living ghost with reasonably friendly words coming in and going out the door. The days were spent as slowly as the settlement money, the late fall and early winter months returning yet again to prove their solidarity with his short days and long nights. A morning after a snowy night, he found himself looking out over the undisturbed expanse of white in remembrance of his days from not so long ago. He didn't much miss the shoveling of the driveway, nor the pain of the shovel pressing against his stomach, nor his father. It was a general missing, as if something had been misplaced. He missed his fingers, he knew. He missed her, too. But an overarching thought never crystallized, never came into focus, a melancholy without an understanding of the melancholic, only a wistful weariness, unarticulated, that lived with him.

Until the thaws of the spring returned. And a new job came to him at a small church, poor and shabby, a large room reserved for the needs of needful and hurt children. There was no proselytizing, no magical mythmaking, no warnings of damnation or conditions, or hypocrisies, only doing the best they could, and a meager pay that he hardly ever took at all. But he knew himself to be lucky, comfortable at home and full, able to give until there was no more to give, and the children, too, understood, and looked upon his two-fifths hand as they would upon their ailments and trepidations, unconsciously and unspoken of. It was a good way to spend the long days and into the night; he didn't mind it at all, the grass in his backyard growing taller still from neglect and disuse, his nights at home spent asleep from a good fatigue, until the small morning hours that took him back. And Sundays were ice cream days.

It was a Tuesday morning when she limped across the church parking lot with a small child in her arms. He watched her from the window drawing closer, expressionless. The he went out to meet her. He can't see and he can't hear, she told him. He looked at the tiny boy in her arms, his eyes open, but not there, his fiery red hair alive and jumping. He looked at her, still the same despite the missed time. He's not yours, she said. He's not yours but I wished he was. She freed a hand to touch his hurt hand.

"God damn. I'll be God damned." He could smile at such clear thoughts.

He gently drew the child from her arms to hold him in his and led her inside to where his many happy children were playing, a space filled with movement and sound, to a place where they could be together for a while.

Follow Me

Sendoff

◆ ◆ ◆

I went [to war] because I couldn't help it.
I didn't want the glory or the pay;
I wanted the right thing done.

Louisa May Alcott, 1863.

ᥱᦺᦂ

I t was raining like it always rains in this part of the country at this time of year, and Jessup Bingham had been standing in the doorway for a while, in thought, breathing in the shifting smells of summer's wet earth. He pushed the screen door open, stepped out on to the porch, and eased the door shut. The rain made a familiar pooling sound against the gravel driveway, and Jessup looked at his watch. He was already twenty minutes behind schedule. Somewhere over the magnolia trees a drape of thunder unfurled, and Jessup looked at his watch again. His wrist dropped. He looked at his worn, tan boots. He took a step forward, then several more to the edge of the porch. His boots now jutted out from under the protective eave, the spill-off breaking its fall against them. He took the stairs, exposing himself in full, the water now drumming and rolling along the thick cotton shirt, his sleeves rolled up along his forearms, the rain forming droplets on the hairs of his exposed arms. His bare head now felt the sting of the falling water. And the cacophony of rain against gravel, flesh, and skull as if in symphony. He took a final step onto the wet, crunchy gravel. Another step. Then more into a trot. Then he began to run. The first lengths were heavy and fraught with a wet cold descending. But the loose gravel and warmth rising propelled him forward. A forward that took him under the canopy of magnolias, magnificent in their sheltering summer repose, and out past the foliage, out toward the street, for a right onto pavement, and on into an opening that drenched his face. Running in full. There were no longer any external sounds, nor like the ones that accompanied him this short distance, but only those interior ones and the things he saw.

He saw things familiar. Mrs. Redwood's porch swing empty, but swaying. And the Lapham twins' tricycles angled sadly and unused on a neglected lawn, waiting for the sun. Liza Firth's "For Sale" sign, there for years upon years, in stubborn defiance of her home's wood rot that had long ago began its consumption. Ignored long enough, it might correct itself. The Detmer house, grand beyond proportion, a sea captain's house with a widow's walk looking out in all directions over the rolling of the lands beyond. Julian and Patty Strobe's Gold

Star centered in the living room window, Chuck's '89 Caprice resting where they had both last worked on it.

When was that? How long ago has it been since he was last here? There's no then and now for a man alone in the world, only a vague recollection of a yesterday, not so indiscriminate from today. A run through the rain like any other day, if it were also raining, only the calendar marking the difference, the old familiars remaining where they'd always be.

The Patterson Middle School playground rests empty, lying fallow until the fall, an old vintage running by it on a rainy August morning, so many years after an earnest children's convocation. And Jessie Bowman's place passes in the way it has always been remembered, neat and hopeful, like her parents, like her, like them together. And Amanda Tillman's place, next over, not as neat, not as hopeful, a father long deserted, leaving behind a daughter of good gratitude for the things she has regardless. They are in the past now, a fleeting desire to glance back defeated by willful concentration. The concentration comes naturally.

Jessup Bingham is paced now. His legs are feeling fire, the pavement almost soft against the weight his body brings to bear. His lungs pump in a discordant rhythm against a rain that continues to fall in full. His hesitancy is passed, his time behind the screen door a quaint reminiscence. Not willful, simply more expedient. He's gaining on his schedule. He can feel it.

His hand wipes against his face. His palms are wetter now, wetness measured in the visceral tension of water forming, holding, then streaming off his fingertips. A wetness akin to plenty, a sensation he might have felt as a child, at the dinner table, full and not wanting any more. His concentration reels, falters, misses a beat. He thinks of the desert. It is a different wetness than a desert wetness. Jessup Bingham's been to the desert, cities and towns in the desert, where the killing takes place. Mostly not by his own volition, but killing just the same. And the heat that makes the body wet, the living and the dead alike. In heavy gear, a heavy sweat from water consumed by the gallon, now salty, drenching and dripping along every extremity and flat surface and making hairs glisten as would an August rain shower, except for the relief. An internal heat escaping, but not relieved.

But there's no time for that. Not now. The road passes still beneath his feet, his head now down, watching the peculiarities and imperfections of well-worn road, the familiar and comforting places passing unnoticed, his legs exhorting exertion, his feet ignoring the pain developing, the mind concentrating on the thing at hand. The running, the breathing, the rain that still falls.

But he must look up, and he does look up. And the Huff acreage passes to the right, row after row after row of controlled nature, corn for livestock, utilitarian fields with secrets held for generations of impatient youth, there sniffing around the garden of adult impersonations. Proving grounds. The memories brighten Jessup Bingham's face, immediate in their effects, his feet still hard against the pavement, the man running past the child, nonetheless a boy running, his face returning to determination, his eyes back to the passing pavement.

He had gone from smallness to the infinite, a world really only seen his way by the very few, not the adventurer, not the humanitarian, not the archeologist sifting through time, and certainly not the avenger or marauder taking at will. He was something else entirely, aware, but hesitant, rueful and protective, heavily armed, but at times improbably helpless, not so unlike this moment unarmed in the rain. There was no searing anger to this helplessness, nor the tautness of frustration. Neither was there fear, or regret. The war would not be lost, even though the dead and disfigured would continue sorrow's work. No, it was none of these.

Jessup Bingham runs, his silent words keeping pace. He had become too big for this place, a bigness measured not in a condescending or invective way. It was in the bigness of words, and those same words applied judiciously to the sights and sounds absorbed deep into the memories of the life being led away from here. And those memories instruct the life being led. The instruction unforgiving, the root in the dark that grows itself downward and outward, all the while pushing all else upward. It was not a common earth into and out of which they all grew. Not anymore. And there was no shame to one way or another. They were but different ways, irreconcilable with neither ease, nor understanding. And there was no shame in that either. But there was shame. There must always be the potential for shame in any individual or collective decision rendered. It's what gives the decision its quality, its very weight. Absent certainty—and there is so little—it's the collective that ought to keep the individual straight and true, even in the muck of barbarity and the weakness of solitude. It is true! It is true! The individual will act heedlessly to preserve sanity; the collective rule-bound and composed. In the collective, there are options. This is what he wanted to believe. In its absence ... Jessup Bingham? He'd shot men no more than boys with seasoned guns in their grips dead.

He ran still. The rain was nothing. Nor were the places and remembrances that sidled by at the feet's pace. There was no here, just as readily as there was no there. There'd be what will be and what could've been—that could've been that could happen again. And it was infuriating, the could've been. And his feet hit the pavement harder, punishing, a warmth still rising despite the cold of the wet, thoughts of the could've-said forming and jettisoning from a harbor long in disorder, a sailing of anger that could lead to nowhere known.

His silent words came in the form of the oratory as soliloquy, before a mass of people, where free men are haunted, but free nations are not. I—we who go—will hold close the same unanswered questions for as long as we stay alive. Do you know what they are? They'll be the only questions of import to our lives. They'll seed the next generation's view of what ought to have been possible. Because within possibility is life. Resist the expedient, the ephemeral. It's a moral imperative to lead this here very life correctly, aware of the consequences of decisions. To say, unequivocally, ten, twenty, thirty years hence that what we did then is right still now. Take courage like courage can only be taken—with the certainty that all else is false. Send us to do the certain thing, send us to a common haunting, when the haunting comes for it will, where death and violence may surely await, but upon our return—and surely some of us are to return—we can say in monuments, and street signs, and common lore that the right thing had been done, lighting those beacons that we knew right from wrong, before it passes from common memory, as it should, to push up what might be next.

Fine words.

There's a hesitancy to Jessup Bingham's running, a slowing of the legs that propel. No thoughts. A concerted respite from that. Just fatigue, hips that ache, a thirsty throat despite the rain that comes. Briefly. He steps harder into his run, his head still down, his right foot fast replacing his left one in a quickening succession. There are people waiting for him in the very same rain, just a distance away. Almost there now, almost together again.

Jessup Bingham's legs took him up a mild grade, working harder still against the expectation of an accustomed habit of flatness, his heart anxious at the sight of the town just within his eyesight, becoming clearer with every effort, every hastened step, a place he'd always been to, a town tired but there. He crested the hill and gravity relieved the tensions against his muscles and feet, running down the equally mild decline now, the rain angled impossibly against his neck, water seeping again down the valley of his spine, like an overtaxed creek at its critical moment. His hand swiped against his back to no effect.

The town is closer, the outlines of milling people taking shape. He'd wanted it that way, the waiting. He'd asked for it this way. His mother, its people's mayor, had resisted. Initially: "I'm afraid it would be inappropriate, unbecoming." His father agreed. The mind is an intransigent place, thought its lubricant. Jessup Bingham had seen too much in the desert. He felt he was in a position to demand. His father fell first, to the simplest of arguments: "Dad, what are you afraid of?" His mother to ancient and oft-repeated sentimentality: "Do I go the way of *dulce et decorum est pro patria mori* wordlessly? Is that all we have left?" She slapped his face hard. Very hard. But he watched her still, ever the officer. Then she retracted and cried, like she knew, his hands forcing the tangled mangrove of her hands in her lap. To be held by her hands for a long while. Then she acquiesced, with the boldest of hopes: "You won't fall."

And Jessup Bingham had his moments at churches, at the high school, at the Rotary and Kiwanis clubs. He spoke to the editor of the *Gazette*, then reread his own words in silence and resignation. He spoke a similar thing in familiar tones because the familiar thing was always new to those who chose to listen: "Killing is effort, sometimes a group one, sometimes a solitary one. I have been trained to kill and I have killed. I kill on your behalf. I am your killer. Yours to do with as you may. And you have made your decisions through your voting and subsequent silence. Those who disapprove do not remain silent. You have asked me to help degrade another people because that is the primary definition of war. The secondary and tertiary definitions of war? It's filth and wallow, sadness and savagery. It's tension and regret, alleviated through hard compassion. It is everything you think you know. And it's nothing

you can know. No words and no images can enhance compre-
hension. Nor me standing here before you with these words.
There's very limited empathy in war. This is not the sympathetic plea of the coward. I am preordained by my profession
to my fate. And there's no honor to my present fate, not in this
fashion, only the kinship of the soldier's love borne of understanding, just like any family undertaking a common journey. Look around you ... your family is right there, too. And
you could never countenance abandonment. And as a nation,
are we not on a common journey? Did we not all—collec-
tively—cry on that violent day in September in what seems
ages and eons ago? Did we not resolve to a common response,
predicated on—rooted in—our notion of justice? There is no
shame in defending ourselves. No people incapable of defense
can ever hope for posterity. But you have allowed our respec-
tive breadth of understanding to part ways. What I know and
what you know are no longer part of a common journey. We
are all off somewhere else. And my mind tells me neither of us
will get to where it is we want to go. And that is a tragedy ...
because we will be a lesser people for it. All of us haunted in
our own separate ways, with nowhere to return to."

No applause. No recriminations. He'd walk away to
silence.

And it was quiet running through the rain. The town's
main street drawing closer. Jessup Bingham was drawing it
closer. The outlines drew crisper. He imagined the muffled
thoughts that awaited him down the line. He had tried ear-
nestly to avoid a tone of sanctimony. He wasn't there to present a sermon to an ultimate truth, nor to cajole. He had

wanted to keep his words to a few, maybe like Lincoln's Second Inaugural or something from Pericles gleaned from his academic days. But he had thought himself ridiculous attempting to mingle the immortal with the mortal. He spoke the best he could, practicing the cadence of his words with his uncertain inner voice as he lay in bed at night, sleepless. Was it the height of temerity to chastise a people for holding fast to a belief, an opinion, to beg them to come with you or not send you at all? He would be there regardless. And coming back in one form or another, regardless. And they would be here, regardless. Jessup Bingham wanted them to know. That's all.

He was there now, at the edge of the commercial district. People lined the sidewalk under umbrellas and hats. A few held signs, others raised their arms as if to wave hello or goodbye, but just seemed to hold them there against the rain. And still others stood nearly expressionless, as if by respectful obligation. He started to pass them, and a shout emerged: "We're with you …", then another: "Godspeed" … and a guttural: "Give 'em hell!" and his mother and father stood under two umbrellas, black and heavy with wetness, his mother smiling, her hand waving at her cheek, his father in solemn salute. And childhood friends—now grown and gaining contentment— looked on knowingly, maybe their years together episodically playing through their memories. A smile left his face for them. And Jessie and Amanda standing side by side, like always, Jessie holding a tiny flag against her breast. She was holding on to something he knew could not be. She did, too, probably, but the conveying words hadn't yet been formulated. Too much lay between now and then, and no words seemed adequate. They loved each other in the old ways, still as sensual because he missed those things. Once this war ended, once he could walk these streets again, they would try to exchange those words. They would be better words than the ones he could use now. They would have a different quality by then. But not now. Not now. Now, he ran onward through the people that stood respectfully watching him.

The crowd thinned. He could see empty spaces along the sidewalk. Main Street was ending. Interest waning. The marginal people of town were here, mostly lethargic men and misunderstood women. Jessup Bingham watched them watching him, both momentary spectacles, fleeting in their novelty, soon to be passed. And he did pass them, and they him, and the street was empty again, of people, but not of the places they'd return to. Jessup Bingham didn't look behind him because he didn't want to know. He ran on, the rain remaining steady, taking a right on Nimitz Avenue and disappearing from any views that may have remained.

By the time Jessup Bingham reached the armory, the rain had stopped. The clouds remained, chaotic and ominous, but the rain was no more. The sergeant major who greeted him met an exhausted man. There was nothing more than silence as the two men stood at an informal attention. Then the sergeant major spoke.

"You have your say, sir?"

"I did. Yes."

Then more silence.

"Your dry gear's inside. We load in ten."

Jessup Bingham turned and walked toward the massive concrete building. The sergeant major looked out after him, then he himself turned and walked toward an empty and idling bus. The first fat drops of a new rain fell, but the sergeant major couldn't be bothered with breaking his stride.

Where She Was, Where She is Going

A Mother's Son

◆ ◆ ◆

It was the ninety-fourth straight day of sunshine. The sun beat down on the Los Angeles basin, hot, but not oppressive. Mrs. Elsa Glavine could be found sequestered in her yard, behind a mid-century Hancock Park bungalow with two years' worth of mortgage left. Twenty-four more payments, mostly equity now. She wanted to be in fine spirits in her summer linens. The garden was looking good; great, actually. The walk had been weeded, ready for another summer, a summer that was proving to be nearly indistinguishable from the spring just passed. The lemon trees smelled like nectar, the hedges along the walls framing the yard abuzz with honey bees working in a pulsating unison, heaving and breathing as if constituting external lungs. The geraniums had been clipped, their chalky detritus in neat piles at their base. The lilacs, succulents, gardenias ... tended-to and in bloom. The jacarandas swayed minutely overhead, not completely succeeding, but not failing entirely in keeping Mrs. Glavine cool and content. She knelt on a soft bed of grass, shortly cut, but lush and comfortable against the knees. She worked the herbs, her hands covered in flecks of her dirt, her earth, alternating snips with sniffs of her worn yellow gloves —of parsley, oregano, mint, cilantro. She worked in silence, her head bent beneath an ancient straw hat given her by her child when he was, in fact, a child, back when she and the mortgage were younger, when time was faster, and the garden not as beautiful.

It had been a good life, and Mrs. Glavine was glad of it.

By mid-afternoon, Mrs. Glavine could be found reclined along the length of a wooden chaise lounge, not asleep, not tired, resting, eyes open skyward. The iron gate by the aza-leas creaked open and a sunny older woman entered. Mrs. Ruthann Snowden. Careful to bring the gate back to rest with thoughtful gentleness, she strolled the walkway, looking about the familiar grounds, walking toward her friend.

"Beautiful day, beautiful day."

Mrs. Glavine nodded, a vagueness attached.

Ruthann Snowden slid into the Adirondack across the chaise lounge and removed her cotton gloves. She reached for the pitcher of vodka and lemonade and poured a tall glass. Remnants of floating ice tolled their last. She drank slowly, the vodka stronger than usual. The woman's eyes watered as they wandered the garden in the lazy delight of admiration.

"A wonderfully beautiful day."

"Roy died last week."

A pause to absorb such words, extended to recollect who Roy may be.

"How do you mean?"

"Car accident. He was ... forty-four."

"Oh, my …" Then no more.

"Forty-three. Dead at forty-three."

Mrs. Glavine wasn't necessarily speaking to her friend, struggling through a tangle of vagueness, memories distant but returning, unsure as to their meeting point, far too many of them to allow for monolithic thought. Her dead son was in there somewhere, the hard-hidden truth of it, the son long abandoned in fact and in memory of a long life. Compulsion's magnetic qualities had had maximal effects on Mrs. Glavine, too tormenting to deny, too intoxicating to ration, the inconvenience of introspection a perfectly repellent charge.

She peered into her tilted glass with a distinct pause laden with expectations and conditions, an implied *quid pro quo* with only one reliable, but forgiving counterparty. Mrs. Glavine was procrastinating, wishing time away, her friend watching her reluctantly, unsure for what to say about the son she'd heard about intermittently, them having never met.

Mrs. Glavine drank.

"I feel I should say something, tell someone something."

Ruthann Snowden nodded, absently, almost obediently.

"About Roy. Say something about him."

Mrs. Glavine despaired of her tenuous position, the nexus between a mother's innateness and the appropriateness of eulogistic redemption. She didn't want to have to talk about this, a conviction she felt in the spasms of her angry hand, the hardness of her pressed lips. It didn't seem just, seemingly a random event, this death, this taking away. Something wanted out from Elsa Glavine, and Ruthann Snowden, bless her heart, was a good listener. She'd listen to anything. For a long time. They were good friends, after all.

"This one's his fault."

Words will come out like that.

"No, I don't mean it like that. Not like that. We've had our misunderstandings. In the past. Things were very different. I at times may not have been the best of mothers to him. But understand, you know, Richard left all those years ago, with that girl. Left me alone with Roy in that miserable desert town. It just wasn't right. Oh, look at me, I'm not composed …"

Ruthann Snowden shook her head, in deep patient commiseration, willing her friend onward. Mrs. Glavine had grown comfortable with taking her time.

"We only had each other. For a long time. But we finally packed it up and left. Just drove out of there one afternoon. It was a Wednesday. And hot, hot. We drove as far as I could."

Mrs. Glavine was quiet for a moment.

"Roy was so helpful. And so quiet in the car. No fussing. I can't remember him even asking for the bathroom. It's funny what you remember."

Ruthann Snowden smiled faintly.

"But we made it to Los Angeles. We made it. I didn't know what we'd do, where we'd go next. But here we were."

Mrs. Glavine looked desultorily around her yard.

"And it wasn't much after that when Bud Long offered me that job, the one … Just dumb luck, really. Met him in that bar … it's gone now. So strange … and …"

Ruthann Snowden leaned forward in her chair.

"… he … well, we all had to do whatever it took back then. I saved a little to buy this house. Put something down. Roy got his own room. You should have seen how happy he was. But he still spent a lot of time alone. Bud moved in with us. It seemed, at the time, to be the best thing for Roy, to give him something—someone—to look up to. And they were fun times, oh my."

Mrs. Glavine adjusted her hat, taking a sip of the drink, noticing the melting ice cubes, taking a longer one.

"That was the first time Roy ran away from the house. Bud brought him back for me. He found him at Union Station. Maybe an hour or two later. He didn't have a ticket. He was just there, on a bench. He and Bud never learned to get along. Very different, those two. It's too bad. Life's too quick. Bud had some good qualities about him. We had our differences. Bud and me. It could have been something. But that was later, when Bud up and left. Roy was grown by then. Almost out of school, sixteen. Working over at Millard's, the butchers. Remember them?"

Ruthann Snowden did.

"Oh, he'd come home a piece. Ohhh!!! I can't tell you how foul … that smell was. His room always had that smell, that … sweet metal smell of blood. Poor Roy. He wasn't too happy there … That must have been around the time I met Bobby Stempenato. Bobby Stempenato … It's funny, his name wasn't even Bobby. It was something different, maybe Angelo. Bobby, he thought it gave him more of an American-sounding name. He was a charmer. It was like living in a cliché, the wine and dance, like something from a different time. We were out almost every night. He was loud. I'll tell you, it would be two in the morning, and he'd be carrying on as if it were noon. You know the type. Full of love for living. Roy ... He left the house and moved to a hotel near work. It gave him more freedom, more time to his own. That's what he told me. I don't know what he did. After work, I mean. I stopped by once. It's funny, I can still see that place of his clearly, him in that small room. You know how that can be ..."

Ruthann Snowden nodded again. She had three grown and gone children.

Mrs. Glavine remained motionless and silent in the tiny hotel room with her son. Was it summer? Were the windows open? Why had she gone? Had she been there before? What did they say to one another? She removed a shirt draped over the back of a chair, folded it neatly against her chest, and replaced it on the seat. And left.

"I sometimes wish I hadn't let go so easily. I don't know if I was holding on very tightly at the time."

Silence.

"Bobby and I didn't last, despite the good times. And I'm not ashamed to say that there were other men after Bobby. And I know Roy didn't approve. I thought we needed a man around the house, a father for him, a husband for me. A family. And Roy didn't approve. Of any of them. And there's only so much a mother can do. But it was too late by then, anyway. Roy was already living at that hotel of his, and maybe he had his friends, and we went about our business. Los Angeles is a big city, we don't just chance across each other in a big city like this. It had to be intentional. And there was a period of time, there, when I may not have seen Roy for a stretch. A long time. I'm not going to keep this from you, Ruthie; these were still hard-playing times. It's just what we did, how it played out. It was too much ... too much of a good many things. My money got took, taken, I had an accident, took a fall. I lost my job, and ... Roy was grown now, had finished his college term, and I had no one else to ask. He came back home. Instead of paying his rent, he paid the mortgage. It made more sense."

Mrs. Glavine waved her hand in a wide arc in the direction of the house. "Part of this is his."

Then more silence.

"He took good care of me. He really did. Bobby and I got reacquainted, he came back to the house, but briefly. And Roy left again. I'd found another job by then. I didn't want Roy to leave. I asked him to stay, but he and Bobby ... He left without saying a word. Just one afternoon, we woke up and he was gone. And gone he stayed. A few years at least. A whir and a blur. Everything racing at once. The oddest time; believe me, Ruthie, when I tell you ..."

Ruthann Snowden nodded her head again, physical punctuation validating sentiment.

"... long nights that melted with the days. As did the job. Or jobs. In Las Vegas, before it got hot out there, I married Tom. This was some time after Bobby had left again. And in Memphis, on our way to Atlantic City we divorced. Or

I think we did. He left me someplace off Beale Street. You can't know shame until something like that happens. I had to borrow the money to call the operator in Los Angeles to connect me to Roy. And he was asleep, it must have been four in the morning. He couldn't understand me at first through the tears and shortness of breath. We spoke on the telephone a long while: 'Slow down, Ma. Slow down.' He just listened and listened. He wired what he could for food and the motel and six days later I met his bus at the station. I don't know why he came all the way out there. I told him I'd make it back on my own. But he came on out anyway. We rode back mostly quietly, sleeping against his arm for mile after mile, wanting to say something but shame getting the better part of me, all the while Roy watching the road passing under the window. Six days of this. Six sober days.

"We stepped off the bus in downtown to a blinding glare. It actually hurt, like God wanting to tell me something urgently and directly. I remember that well. I looked over at Roy to see if his eyes were having the same ... revelation to the light as mine. But I didn't see anything different. He had the same undisturbed eyes, my bags filling his hands, leading me to the cab stand. We were going home."

Home.

"It was going to be different. I promised myself."

The sun was high, high in the blue sky, its warmth immediate. The women were quiet for a moment before Ruthann Snowden spoke.

"Elsa. All these years ..."

"That was before our time.

"Yes …"

"We were home again. And it felt like a home, just the two of us for as long as Roy could stay. Just the both of us. And I wanted him to stay, the way a mother wants her son to stay. But living gets in the way. It just does, Ruthie. He took a place in Long Beach," and Mrs. Glavine waved her hand before her face, dismissively. "He knew I didn't have a car."

She looked at her hands, then placed them carefully in her lap, an elegant woman of manners. In a whisper, she said, "I asked him, before he left that one time, why he keeps doing what he does for me. I didn't want him to think I didn't know. He didn't answer. A letter arrived in the mail sometime later."

Mrs. Glavine removed a folded envelope from her pocket, removing its single sheet content, white and creased. "I read it again this morning."

She unfolded the letter and read Roy's words aloud: "'*The Mother is the soil. At her cruelest, she can be barren and the taker of life, but she gave original life and hope keeps us rooted to her.* How's that, Ma? I know how much you've come to love your garden. We give what we may have and take what is given. That's all there could ever be. I guess we have no right to expect anything more. I hope this answers your question.'"

Mrs. Glavine refolded the paper, replacing it in its envelope, and let it drop into the folds of her dress that formed in her lap.

"That's how he'd become, good with his words, without my noticing. He'd never written me a letter before." There was neither pride, nor hurt, nor resignation in her latest words. Only words as narrative, a woman with a story to be told. "Nothing came of it. We still spent our time apart. He found his way to Santa Barbara. His son had come. I understood."

Ruthann Snowden nodded again.

"There's always things to be done, and always a next thing …"

"Always the next thing," Ruthann Snowden said in rumination.

"But Ruthie, I didn't think it would be like this. I never would have imagined an ending, if it were up to me. A mother shouldn't have to let go of her son."

Ruthann Snowden wanted to stand, to take her friend's hand in hers, to act. She didn't stir.

"No, she shouldn't."

A silence became two, one for each.

"We've let go of each other to live in two different worlds. He came back to mine many more times than I went to his. I know. It's how we were. That's the people we were. I imagine him as that little boy, out there somewhere becoming the man, I imagine him out on that road alone … "

A fattening tear gestated delicately where the eye's softness ends and the high cheekbone begins. Ruthann Snowden watched it, almost holding her breath, waiting for it to cascade. It fought to stay in place instead.

"Why are we the people that we are, Ruthie? How does it come out this way? How come we don't have no say in it, like we're just along for the ride? I've come to want to know. It only seems right to want to know."

Mrs. Glavine picked up the glass, the ice melted, the liquid tepid, useless to her.

"I don't know how to end it. I don't know what to do. I'm no one's mother now. Who does that make me? Who do I become, Ruthie?"

Ruthann Snowden couldn't know.

Mrs. Glavine stood with a quickness, the letter falling from the folds of her dress. She walked down the path, stopping suddenly, returning. She stood above Ruthann Snowden.

"I imagine him out on that road alone, up in those hills. That long way he had to come and go back. I'd asked him to come back to come get me, to go see that boy of his, my grandson. He said he'd come. But I couldn't go. Something came up at the very last minute. I left him a note on the door. I left the backdoor unlocked. Food in the fridge. Told him I'd be back as soon as I could. I thought he'd wait. I said I was sorry. But he left, went back away."

She tuned back down the path, fondling the leaves of a wilting flowering bush. "You know, Ruthie, I wish it would rain in this goddamned place once in a while. It would save me some time in watering these things."

She crossed the compact lawn and knelt at a newly planted hydrangea. She dug at the earth, pouring water from a plastic jug, patting at the roots. Ruthann Snowden looked out after her, before leaning forward to retrieve the envelope from the ground. She placed it on the table, and started to rise to excuse herself.

What sets man apart from the beasts
is that humans have the option not to panic.

Victor Serge, *Unforgiving Years*

Continuity, Interrupted

Panic

◆ ◆ ◆

Umm Quassem awoke with the dawn. A bit afterward, actually. She was getting older. Her husband wouldn't stir despite great noise, she knew, but she slipped out from under the covers as quietly as she could. Abu Quassem didn't stir. She found her matted plush slippers where she'd left them the night before, slipping into them, and moved from the bedroom door, along her route to the kitchen.

It was hot already and every window remained in a position to receive any breeze the jealous Tigris deemed ready to exhale. If it would, this would be the time of day. The kitchen drapes moved imperceptibly at either side of the window.

She took the plump oranges from the hanging mesh bag and placed them on the counter by the sink. She washed and rinsed one after the other under a surprisingly powerful torrent of water gushing from a hissing faucet. She dried the oranges with a soft blue towel of Egyptian cotton. She opened a drawer to the left of the sink and removed a sharp knife with a glossy wooden handle. She wiped the knife absently with the towel, and effortlessly cut each orange nearly symmetrically in half. She reached to her right for the white plastic juicer, placing it fittingly atop a large glass container, and brought the orange halves to its pointed summit, and with remarkable upper-arm and wrist strength, ground and ground and ground and ground juice and pulp into the receptacle. She placed the spent fruit to one side, reached for two tall glasses resting at an angle on the metal drying rack.

She repeated her actions twenty more times, filling the glass container. She lifted it, moved across the kitchen to the standing icebox, opened it, and placed it in the darkened interior. She removed four eggs from a flat ceramic dish. She tapped the door closed.

She moved to the iron stove and moved a frying pan from one burner to another. She reached for a bottle of olive oil, opening it, tilting its contents into the base of the pan. Replacing the bottle, she turned a metal switch, waited, turned a knob, and struck a wooden match. Circular fire.

She waited in place.

The oil in the pan snapped—a light snap. She stepped forward, reaching for the eggs, cracking each one in turn against the steel lip, easing their contents in the hot oil. Snap. Pop. Snap. Pop. The cracked shells, she placed in a plastic bowl. From a small glass jar, she sprinkled sumac on the frying eggs, each in their turn.

In the distance, a thump. Followed in quick succession by several more. Then silence again. Umm Quassem poked at the eggs, moving them clockwise. She moved back to the sink, removing an oval pink sponge, wetting it under a trickle of water from the faucet. Her gaze wandered out through the dancing drapes. She moved back across the kitchen floor to a square plastic table against the wall. Three wood and straw chairs. She chased around a full fruit bowl as she vigorously wiped the tabletop, the streaks of water glinting in the sun that had finally penetrated the window, the bowl finding its final resting place in the corner.

Back at the sink, she rinsed the sponge and drew the thin cloth curtain across the window. She removed two stone plates form the drying rack and moved back to the stove. She extinguished the flames. She removed a spatula from its holder and deftly lifted two eggs on each plate. She retraced her steps back to the table, placing the plates on opposite sides. She moved back near the stove, taking two forks, two paper napkins, the salt and pepper shakers. She placed the collection in the center of the table. From atop the icebox, she retrieved a basket of flat bread and a small, thin glass bowl of green olives floating in oregano-flecked olive oil. She placed these on the table, against the wall. She turned and opened the icebox, removing two frosty glasses and the container of squeezed orange juice. She placed the glasses alongside each plate, and the orange juice in the middle.

She turned and walked back toward the kitchen door, peered out into the hallway, and bellowed:

"Quassem! Abu Quassem! Where are you?"

She moved back toward the stove, removing the pan to the sink. Soap suds were forming, collecting under the running water when two men—one young, one old—entered the kitchen and moved directly to the table.

"Morning," muttered the older man.

Umm Quassem didn't turn to look.

"Come here so I can look at you."

The young man rose off his chair and went to his mother's side. She wiped her hands on the towel draped over the sink's edge, and grabbed her son by the back of his neck, driving her lips into his cheek. Then, just as forcefully, released him.

"May you bury me, God willing. Go eat."

The young man returned to the table and eased into the chair. His father, hunched over his plate, didn't look up. He slowly dipped a torn piece of bread in the yolk of the egg. The son tore his bread in half, placed his elbows on the table, leaned in, and gingerly poked at his yolk until it ruptured. A viscous yellow streamed onto the plate. Father and son ate in hunched silence, serenaded by the scrubbing sounds of a metal brush against a metal pan.

By the time Umm Quassem had finished cleaning her cooking area and returned to sit on the middle chair at the table, the men were picking at the green olives. Their cleaned plates were speckled with coarse pits. Umm Quassem wiped at the corners of her mouth watching her son. The old man pushed his chair back, standing, lifting his plate, moving to the sink, placing it on the counter. He turned the faucet on, washed his hands and washed his lips. He reached for the towel, his wife now watching him.

"Not that one. The other one."

Abu Quassem dried his mouth and hands. His son rose and followed suit, reaching for the anointed towel. A military helicopter, then two more, fluttered into view in the near distance. The young man peered through the translucent drapes at them until they were gone, their sounds quickly fading to silence.

"Let's go." Abu Quassem was at the kitchen's doorway. Umm Quassem remained hunched over the table, picking at the remaining olives. Her son moved to her and kissed her lightly atop her head.

"What's for dinner?"

"Chicken and rice."

Quassem moved toward his father.

"God be with you," she said, her voice carrying over her shoulder.

There was no response, just slow footsteps down the hallway. A heavy metal door opened, then gently clicked shut. Umm Quassem reached into the fruit bowl and removed an orange. She cut the fruit along near-symmetrical lines from top to navel, six cuts, peeling back the skin, bringing each in turn to her nose before eating, inhaling deeply each time.

The morning had found its midpoint. The city baked, the little house with the heavy metal door baked, and Umm Quassem moved slowly about her work. The beds had been made, the laundry placed in the agitating machine, the front stoop swept, when the explosion happened. It had been in the distance, muffled against interspersed concrete and space found across distance and neighborhoods, its reverberations rattling the windows, and it may have been a Baghdad common place, but there was a proximity to it, an instinctive closeness. She had been in the kitchen again, holding a knife, preparing to slice an onion. She replaced the knife on the counter and moved toward the hallway, then toward the living room, the room where the heavy metal door kept the world out. She stood at the window, its heavy fabric drapes drawn, the glass panels pushed outward. She looked through the wrought-iron bars to watch a dreamy scene unfold—women emerging uncertainly from doorways, congregating and congealing in clumps along the sidewalk, methodically, body language betraying initial whispers that led to loud talking, then bodies turning to gaze in the direction of the vanished sound, now replaced by discordant sirens. More women emptied out into the street from doorways unseen, the congregations growing larger, louder, Umm Quassem watching, unmoving, then wails and individual departure: "Hurry! Hurry! Something has happened!" Then mass movement. Umm Quassem moved to the heavy metal door, unlocking it, opening it, taking her first tentative steps into her new day. She looked out after the women, and more came streaming by, then more and more. The smell of burning diesel hung in the still air of the fluid neighborhood, not so uncommon, yet different, sweeter somehow. She took two steps off the stoop and looked to her right—black, unnatural smoke rose and rose, then dissipated high, high among the blue of a cloudless sky. She was on the sidewalk when a young woman in a bathrobe brushed by her, wordless, her heavy panting as audible as her heavy barefooted steps. Umm Quassem began walking quickly in the direction of the migrating women. Her legs were no longer controlled by her brain, her eyes usurping all neural energy to focus on the billowing smoke on the near and imminently reachable horizon. Something else moved her legs forward in seemingly shocking rapid succession.

Umm Quassem wasn't designed to run. She had never run in her adult life, the wonderment of the childhood frolic not part of her remembrance. But she ran, her light blue 'abaya restricting, constricting, but she ran. Silently and directly. She ran. Her lungs hurt. Her ankles hurt. Her head hurt, her eyes tearing, her brow glistening, then beading with a heavy sweat. There were women in front of her, behind her, along parallel and perpendicular streets she could not see, coming from all directions, a convergence of women because they all knew where their men would be.

How far does a body run to meet its destiny? An hour? A day? A fortnight? A lifetime? There could be no preparation for what awaited Umm Quassem, only the slowing of the body and the racing of the heart, a wading through proverbial chaos, a languid movement among the seemingly immovable, both living and torn apart, the mind filtering and sorting, filtering and sorting, searching for guidance and sanity ...

Oh ... who are we? Who are we that do such things to one another? What wellhead of hatred have we tapped to return to such a state? What pitiless plague has been unleashed at the dawn of the harvest? Why are we so alone on the banks of a rising river? Why do we not move? Why can we not move? Umm Quassem waded through other people's tragedy, looking for her own. The sounds of modern machines and primitive wailing ushered in a new reality, a new life, a dark-ened brooding one where hopelessness triumphs at its brutal whim. Umm Quassem's now bare feet were smeared in the blood of generations, the soles of her feet cut and rutted by sharp objects beneath the flotsam of blood and debris, and desperate voices rising:

"Umm Quassem! Umm Quassem! They have killed these good men. Killed them for waiting for a job. They have killed them all. Where are you, God?"

It was the voice of a neighbor, a friend, a woman her age with two boys and a husband. But only the voice reached her as she plodded forth, lurching and stumbling forth on unthinking instinct, tearless, looking down at the right exact moment to find her men in a godless state, nearly side by side, twisted and contorted, pain and gasping on their faces, flesh bared to an unremitting past-noon sun. She knelt, her 'abaya settling into the pooled blood, soaking it upward into its thirsty cotton fabric. She touched her son's face, then her husband's hand, his wedding band still shiny. Then she gently eased herself atop them both.

Flights of Fancy

Juicy, Doucement

◆ ◆ ◆

"**H**ey Juicy, wait up." That would be Amy Zahn, waving crazily, running like a little brunette lunatic across the grass. I keep walking. Besides, I don't answer to that nickname anymore.

"Ohhh Jay … Come on. Slow up." Those little legs are sure moving now. But I have to get home, so I don't have time for petite Amy Zahn. Although she is a very nice person. We've been friends since the first grade. I keep walking.

"Odessa Jean. Hey!" I stop and turn. She's still running, in full sprint, getting closer and noisier. She just might run through me or right on by. I find myself wondering how many feet it will take her to come to a complete stop. And in an instant, she's there. Panting.

"Don't call me that," I say and start walking again.

"Call you," she says huffing, "what?" She concludes puffing, following closely behind.

"Odessa Jean."

"Well, you weren't hearing Juicy or O.J." She's at my side now.

"I heard you."

"Oh."

I'm back up to my pre-Amy pace.

"Did you want to come over later?"

"Not today. I can't."

We walk along in silence. It's a nice day. I like the fall, but not as much as I love the spring, when everything seems so new.

"Are you excited?" Amy again.

"About what?"

"Your Dad."

"Of course."

Some questions are more stupid than others. But it's spring and my father is coming home. So I don't mind. We keep walking at my pace.

"Well, okay. I guess I'll take off home, too."

"Okay, Amy. I'll see you in school on Monday."

"Want to do homework together this weekend?"

"I'll see you on Monday."

And with that, Amy stops along the sidewalk.

"Bye, Juicy."

I wave to her, but she only sees the back of my hand. I wasn't trying to be rude. I really do like Amy. It's just that I really need to be home. I'll make it up to her next week.

The door is open and the house smells like cooking. I can hear the hissing of the pressure cooker from the kitchen.

"Hi Mom!"

I place my bag on the chair in the hallway. My mother walks in from the kitchen. She looks cute in her apron, sandals, and bandana.

"You look cute."

"Aren't you sweet."

She's looking around the hallway. I can tell her mind is preoccupied, her thoughts probably ticking off the list of things she has yet to do.

"Is there anything you need me to do down here?"

"No, I don't think so. I don't think so."

I pick the bag up. "I'll be upstairs."

"You don't want your father to see your room a mess, do you?"

I climb the stairs as my mother returns to the kitchen. I'm not hungry at all.

By any honest measure, my room is a mess—piles of newspapers, books, magazines, color pencils, pens, scissors, clipping shreds, empty bags, stuffed bags of ripped-up paper, stuff. I've been made aware of the mess on several occasions. I keep one area clutter-free, over by the desk, but there are plates with crumbs there, too. I pile them up and take them downstairs every few days. But that's still a day off yet. The book bag slips off my shoulder and thumps against the carpeted floor. Poor books. I tiptoe through the junk and ease right on into the desk chair. It's a big desk. I could sleep on it, even, and not have to worry about rolling off. The computer's on, like it's always on, and the printer hums or buzzes, like it always does. I've been waiting for it to die since I was in middle school, and now I'm in the tenth grade. They don't make things as disposable as they used to.

I move the keyboard out of the way and drag a big hand-made cardboard-bound scrapbook across the tabletop. I open to the first page. It's pink, the page. There's Dad smiling as he does when he forgets someone's watching him. And Mom, too, is there. I've stenciled flowers all along the edges of the paper. It's a nice opening page, I think.

I turn pages. At the winter break play last year, lots of empty beach scenes, calm waters, but the stenciling on these aren't as good, the lines aren't good, and the colors are all wrong. But once it's on, it's on. Dad alone at the front door, ready. I cut and paste black-and-white insignia of his 11th Marine Expeditionary Unit from a military website. I think it's the right one. I forgot to ask him before he left. We took a family picture outside the house before we got in the car to say goodbye. That was a nice one. We didn't take a picture of him after that. We drove in silence, said one more goodbye, and drove back home.

I didn't have to be told where he was going. Or what it meant. I already knew all that. He came up to the room any-way, knocked, came in, and sat on the bed. I was at the desk. He told me about Iraq, its importance to this country, how sometimes it's better to think ahead than to regret later.

"You don't like to regret things, do you, Odessa Jean?"

"I don't think so."

Of course, I didn't, he said, nobody does. And it's true, nobody does.

It wouldn't take long because it couldn't take long. There were too many other things to do afterward. It's best to do one thing at a time. Straight down the line. I wouldn't do my French homework and my math at the same time, would I?

I'd never thought about it, so I said *non, jamais.* So there'd be nothing to worry about. It would be a memory soon, something we could remember together. I can do, and you can start the remembering part. I liked that idea. And you can send me letters with any questions you can come up with. Just in case something doesn't want to make sense. Okay, I can do that. And I could. I liked writing letters. And, the more I think about it, maybe the best way for us to remember together is for you to keep track of it for us. There'll be stories coming back in magazines and newspapers and on the news about what we're doing. It'll be hard to hide out there in the desert. It'll be like you're there, too. You keep a diary of the news for us. And when I come back, we'll go through it together. Like a yearbook? Something like that, lots of pictures, some words. Whatever you want to make of it. But save that last page for the two of us. We'll put just the right pictures and words on that last page together. Then we'll put it on the bookshelf. I could see it up there on the bookshelf in the living room. Then we won't have to worry about those types of things again.

I wondered how I'd make the binding and what title I'd put on the cover. I would need lots of colored paper and specialty pens for this project. That much I did know.

Dad took me to the hobby store and got me what we needed. I punched holes in the papers wide enough for wide pieces of red yarn to flow through them. The cover and back were thick cardboard, the front with a protective plastic covering. I stacked the blank papers and cardboard and threaded the yarn through. I tied a tight bow in the back. And waited.

That was before he left eighteen months ago. And even after he left, nothing much happened. I started to fill the blank pages of the book with pictures I'd taken with the camera I'd gotten for Christmas. I had one of Mom coming out of the shower, but she made me delete it before I could paste it in the book. Then she took the camera away for a while. But after the war had started, I didn't need the camera so much anymore. It was March and it was dark out. And I got ready to get busy.

We were told the war had started. There were cameras there. And an email to make the war ours came the same night: "I won't be able to send anything for a while. I'll see you at the other end." I cut and pasted his short note on the very last pink page. The newspaper came big and bold and stuffed with what I needed daily from Los Angeles right to the door and two weekly magazines came by mail on Monday. Sometimes Tuesday. The newspapers I could cut up that evening, but I had to wait for the end of the week before I could have my way with the magazines. I liked the shiny magazine paper better, but the newspapers had better and bigger headlines and maps with arrows. The scrapbook would end up having tons of inky fingerprints all over the place. They looked to me artsy, though, so I stopped trying to erase them or draw over them. Inky thumbprints are a good starting point for paisley prints. I learned that from a scrapping book. So the pages have colonies of colorful amoebae slithering about. It adds more than it takes away.

There was too much information, too many maps and arrows; diagrams and illustrations; history and opinions;

cartoons and letters; newspapers and magazines; the evening news and the afternoon news; the Internet and links that went further and deeper; pictures and videos, pictures and videos, pictures and videos. I followed the arrows across the map, read long and interesting articles, knew when sandstorms swept across the desert's floor, looked at dead people in ditches, saw things burning and people running and crying.

I didn't know what to include, what he'd like for us to remember. Nothing said it neatly. Or clearly. The big headlines in the newspapers made the most sense, the biggest news piece of the day. In the *Los Angeles Times*, at least. And pictures from there on the front page, they seemed important. But it doesn't tell a whole story, not really. There were other things I couldn't include. I cut and saved, always with the idea of coming back later and adding what seemed to be missing. But more kept coming in. I couldn't keep up. I had my routine, after school and on the weekends. One day, one page.

I have five hundred and sixteen pages in all, each numbered in the bottom right-hand corner. The five hundred and seventeenth page is blank.

I open the book and turn past the pink pages to the first of the blue war pages, where the stories I'd chosen for us to remember are, a few from many, many, for the umpteenth time, a daily ritual it seemed, every day remembered in its way.

I turn the blue pages to see where I'll be today:

<u>March 20</u> **U.S. Attacks Iraq**: *War to Oust Hussein Begins with Airstrikes*

Orange pictures of their city at night with flames and smoke. And a map of the country. I had added a note at the bottom wondering how in the wide world anyone could possibly survive this kind of thing. Are their houses made of wood, too?

∾o∾

<u>March 21</u> **Ground Attack Begins**: *16 Killed in Helicopter Crash Are First Allied Deaths of War.*

I couldn't find a picture of the helicopter crash. And I didn't want to, either. There are a few pictures of tanks and trucks lined up and a map diagrammed with arrows. I wondered how the mothers of those dead soldiers felt, how sad they must have been. I drew sixteen daisies at the bottom of the page.

∾o∾

<u>March 23</u> **Resistance Slows Troops as They Head Toward a Battered Baghdad**

There seems to be a lot of walking in war. I have several pictures of people—old, young, soldiers—walking somewhere.

∾o∾

<u>March 30</u> – **Suicide Blast Kills 4 GIs at Checkpoint**

I didn't know what this meant. I do now. I pasted a very sweet picture of a soldier holding a girl. She looks very young, three or four, maybe. I don't think she was hurt.

∽∽

<u>April 1</u> – **Allies Pound Iraqi Guard Near Capital**

I have a picture of a woman on a bridge. She is sitting on the pavement, looking at a soldier. She looks scared. The caption says she had been caught in a crossfire on the bridge in Hindiyah. The town in right on the Euphrates, midway between Al Hillah and Karbala. I marked it on my wall map.

∽∽

<u>April 2</u> – **U.S. Troops Break Through Iraqi Lines; POW Is Rescued.** *As Combat Escalates, Sparing Civilians Gets Harder, Too*

An American girl-soldier had been captured, but she was rescued. I think the country was relieved. I also have a picture of a 155-millimeter self-propelled howitzer firing on enemy positions. In the distance.

∽∽

<u>April 4</u> – **U.S. Tightens Noose on Baghdad**

I didn't like the imagery of this headline. I still don't.

∽∘∾

<u>April 7</u> – **U.S. Seizes Presidential Palaces**: *'We Own Baghdad,' a Colonel Says as Iraqi Resistance Dwindles*

I have a picture of a long line of trucks along a canal, or stream, on fire. The canal, that is. Water burning!

∽∘∾

<u>April 10</u> – **Baghdad in U.S. Hands**: Symbols of Regime Fall as Troops Take Control

And sure enough, there is a picture of a statue being pulled to the ground. I also have a picture of people going crazy in the streets in what the newspaper says was "a spree of celebration and looting." I think I have a picture of the looters. But they could be both. It's still hard to tell.

∽∘∾

<u>April 12</u> – **To Wary Baghdad Shopkeepers, 'Liberation' Looks Like a Jungle**

This one was very true. I couldn't find a happy picture of anyone, anywhere over there. Not on that particular day, at least.

I tried. So I have those pictures of wary-looking Baghdad shopkeepers.

∽o∽

April 13 – Ancient Wonders Are History as Mob Plunders Iraq Museum

I think they even took the sinks from the bathrooms. That's what the newspaper said. Can you imagine?

∽o∽

April 21 – In the Wake of War, Sorting Out the Dead: *Many Iraqi bodies were hastily buried in shallow ditches after fighting ended. Volunteers are helping families identify their missing relatives.*

I don't know why I cut this story out. I think I pasted it in before I really thought about it. I could've removed it. I still could. But I didn't. And I won't. There's a picture of two men looking into the back of a pickup truck with high walls, like an open-air hearse stacked with bodies. They're crying.

∽o∽

May 2 – Bush Hails Victory in Iraq

I don't think this was true.

∽o∽

<u>May 2</u> – **Hospitals Gutted, Medical Care Takes to Streets**

The only day in which I have two pages. I cut this story out because I'd started volunteering twice a week (after school) at Mom's hospital. I have a picture of soldiers treating injured or sick people. I could imagine myself there, helping. I'd stick to what I know. I'd help children. Although I didn't cut out any pictures of wounded kids.

<u>May 3</u> – **Home at Last**

This is one of my favorites. It's a very simple and clean page. In the center of the page, there's a picture of two sailors on an aircraft carrier in their dress whites. One of the sailors has a huge smile on his face. The caption says that he's smiling because one of them has just spotted his wife and four children.

<u>July 21</u> – **Marriage Missing in Action:** *Jennifer Bowers makes do at home as Scott, her husband, soldiers on in Iraq. After 10 months, there's still no light at the end of their tunnel.*

I showed Mom this article before I pasted it in the book. She didn't say anything about it. I didn't ask. At least we weren't alone in how we were feeling.

November 13 – **Deadly Iraqi Blast Targets Italian Police**

This was in Nasiriyah, south of the capital along one of the rivers. A real mess. Italy was starting to wonder what it was doing over there in the first place. I found an English-language Italian website and read about it. I have a picture of the Italian prime minister with his hands formed as if ready for prayer.

∽o∾

December 26 – **Antiwar Family's Conflict** *Fervent peace activists sort through complex emotions as they mourn son killed in Iraq. He died a hero, they say – a parents' contradiction*

"I know it seems like a contradiction. How can your son be a hero in an unjust war?" This is what the father asked in the article. I thought about him and just war, wondering if anyone has ever said they want to start an unjust war. How do wars start? Where do they come from? That was the better question, I thought, the one on my mind. I haven't found the answer yet.

∽o∾

February 10 - **With Rotation, Troops in Iraq to Get Grayer** *A greater proportion of the replacement forces are older than 40. The military hopes their experience and maturity will be assets*

They looked tired, too. I thought of my father; his birthday would be in two days, wondering if anyone out there with him would remember. Maybe wish him a happy birthday. I sent him a card with my letter that week.

☙✦❧

<u>March 11</u> – **U.S. Combat Fatalities in Iraq Surge Suddenly** *After a recent lull, nine troops die in five days. Officials say it's too early to discern a trend*

When I leaf back through the scrapbook, day by day, I definitely see a discernible trend. It's more like a constant.

☙✦❧

<u>April 14</u> – **Slain Soldier's Two Sisters Grieve** *The woman's military siblings weigh whether to return to Iraq or stay home in Wisconsin*

Their option came too late. I wished all three sisters had stayed home, there in Brookfield, Wisconsin. I found some pictures of the town on the Internet. It looks very nice, even with all that snow in winter.

☙✦❧

<u>May 10</u> – **Another Tour of Anxiety for Troops' Kin** *Families struggle to cope as soldiers in a New England Army reserve unit have their stays in Iraq extended for a second time*

May is my favorite month. I always hope for good things in May.

☙✦❧

<u>May 11</u> – Iraqi Women Describe Abuse in Custody, Stigma Afterward

"I hope it's not true, because were it to be true, it is just too horrible to imagine." I hoped it wasn't true, too.

❦

<u>May 12</u> – U.S. Businessman Beheaded in Iraq as Militants' Videotape Rolls

I pasted a still image from the video, grainy and very scary. A moment from right before. The video was posted on the Internet. I found it. But that's all I did.

❦

<u>July 20</u> - A Father Mourns in Baghdad

This day, only a photograph, a father bent over a stretcher in a hospital. His twenty-year old son had been killed in a suicide truck bombing. He died with lots of others. That's what the caption says.

❦

<u>August 23</u> – No End to the Violence in Najaf

I have a pink pushpin on the map where Najaf is. It's a holy city. Dad is there.

❦

<u>September 16</u> – **Many Faces, One Heartache** *From coast to coast, families are torn over love and patriotism as the list of Iraq war dead grows*

The picture I have is a woman holding her baby, born a few days after her husband died. The baby is a boy. Very cute, sleeping there in her arms. "I just don't know what to think. Part of me wants to support the war, but part of me doesn't." I can imagine which thought will win out.

⤜∘⤏

And that's it, maybe thirty days of five hundred and sixteen, the next and last page blank. Our eighteen months had found themselves whole. I didn't want to stop. It would have been a story without an end, hanging out there by itself. I did, finally, the day after Dad told us he's on his way home. An early morning phone call. That was a week ago. It was over now. For us. And our book complete. As much as the temptation to go back and make changes was there, like today, I didn't do it. And I really, really wanted to do it. I had a great many ideas, so many other ways to make it different. But it had been Dad's idea. And we'd been doing it together, really, him there and me here. I couldn't go back and change things. Just like he couldn't. I didn't think memories ought to be edited.

I could've asked him about it, but I didn't. Besides, Dad hadn't written me as many letters as he said he would. They came, but not that often. I got many more short emails. It was easy enough to understand, him not writing in longhand.

When I wrote him my letters, and I did do it once a week, every Friday night, I had mostly questions on my mind, and I tried to put them into context for him, in the same way I'd been thinking about them. I wrote him long letters (I was once up until Saturday dawn writing the same letter). And they got longer the longer he was away, the way thoughts get longer -

"Odessa, come down quick," Mom's voice comes straight down the hallway and takes a right into the room.

I quickly slide off the chair and am down those stairs in no time. The banister acts as the fulcrum, and I'm on the double-quick down the hallway to the kitchen. I go from the hallway's dim lighting to the kitchen's florescent one to see my mother beaming like a fool and my father leaning against the sink. And stop. A moment tossed into the air, waiting to come back again.

"Odessa Jean? Come here!"

I don't think I thought, I just go. I don't remember moving along the white speckled tile, only his arms around my head pressing against his neck. Goodly, tightly. For the longest moment. Then away and a kiss to the forehead. Then back in again, his hand going against the grain of my hairs. Then out again, at a long arm's length, then release and a smile.

We three stand there on the speckled tile floor in silence.

"I have something for you," I say.

"Okay!"

I turn and ran from bright to dim, the fulcrum again, up the stairs two at a time, to the room, to the desk, the book slammed shut and off the desk, and on down again.

In the kitchen, they're at the breakfast table. The book goes between them, pushed leftward toward Dad.

"It's done. It's for you. The last page is blank."

Dad opens the book and turns the pages.

"I tried to get every story from every day. But there were too many. So I slowed down a little bit, around here," turning the pages to an almost random page. "Or someplace. Do you remember this here?"

I turn the page.

"Each page has a different design on the frame, see?"

I turn more pages.

"And these paisley things are from my thumbprints. But some pages are from magazines, so there isn't any paisley drawing," turning more pages until a glossy and clean image looked out at us. "These were always better ones to work with, but I couldn't find enough of them. See here, I put a newspaper one and a magazine one on the same page. See the difference?"

"Juicy, *doucement. Doucement.* I know you know what that means. Just … Not now." My father closes the book.

I look at him as he looks away, wait, take the book and leave the kitchen.

Dad is up in my room. I knew he was regretting how he said what he'd said. He didn't need to, but he did. He sits on the end of the bed again and looks around the room. I sit at the desk and watch his eyes wander.

"On pardonne tant que l'on aime. Do you know that one?"

I don't, but I nod anyway. I'll piece it together later with the French-English dictionary.

"I should've said things differently. And I'm sorry. I'm a little tired, that's all. We'll get to all those things. Just not tonight."

"I know."

His eyes wander the room again.

"I see you've gotten yourself some pretty detailed maps." He stands and walks to the wall, leaning in for a closer look.

"I did."

"Najaf in pink."

"I got then online. I borrowed Mom's credit card. I know all about geography now."

"Did they come in those thick cardboard tubes?"

"They did. I saved them just in case I ever had to draw a map or something like that."

"You never know."

He turns and comes back from the wall. He sits on the bed again.

"There'll be time later for all the hard work you did. We'll look through it together. I promise. You're older now, you understand better. You can imagine someone not wanting to think about something right just yet."

"Yes."

He looks back at the wall map for a time.

"It doesn't feel like we had anything to do with any of that, the green river that flows the way it's shown. Easy, right on up. Not even during the war part early on, on the move along those highways. The part that's the easiest to understand. The parts there on your map. It's none of that. We ended up in places not on your map, reacting to things that kept happening to us, like being inside a giant paper bag with someone on the outside hitting it with a stick. Just sudden and always. Not knowing when, but the swinging stick ready at any time. We wanted to get on with it, have a real war, terrible to say I know, and get out of that paper bag. Finish it. Go home. Do something else."

He's quiet for the longest time, a little happy smile on his face, like he's trying to remember an old joke that probably wasn't all that funny.

"It was like doing chores on a Saturday morning. Being there. If you can imagine. It's funny. The afternoon couldn't come soon enough. But can you also imagine the afternoon ruined by rain? Always ruined by the rain. It rained all the time. In torrents and sheets. And this sticky, gloopy mud formed. Everyplace and everywhere. All the time. Our afternoon sun just wouldn't come. We tried to keep each other as safe and dry as best we could. Inside the bag. The inside of that bag was all we had to look forward to, coming out of the rain as we did. That's where I read your letters. And I loved your letters, Odessa Jean. I'm sorry for being so slow in writing back. I wrote back when I could. I wrote when the pen felt *just* right against the paper. Just right. I loved writing those letters. I hope you liked them, too."

I nod. I loved his letters, too.

"Sometimes—just sometimes—there's very little to say. You've had times like that. You know. Something wants to come out, but something else knows better. Keeps it quiet instead. So I was quiet for a lot of the time. Whenever I could.

I missed you for every moment. It was the hardest thing to do. And the easiest thing to do. If that makes sense."

It made sense. I missed him as well.

He leaves the room without anything more.

I stand and walk to the map on the wall. I, too, lean in for a closer look at the brown and beige tones and the strip of green along the flat river valley. I did know my geography. It hadn't occurred to me that it rained that much in that part of the world. It just hadn't.

Now I know.

About the Author

♦ ♦ ♦

Ramzi's approach to fiction is influenced by Chandler, Orwell, and Vonnegut: keep it emotional, be direct, have fun doing it. *guttersnaps* is the result. This is his first book. He lives in Charleston, SC with his wife and two children.